Never Meant to Fall for You

B. Lane

Copyright © 2023 B. LANE
Published by T'Ann Marie Presents, LLC
All rights reserved. No part of this book may be reproduced in any form without written consent of the publisher, except brief quotes used in reviews. This is a work of fiction. Any references or similarities to actual events, real people, living or dead, or to real locals are intended to give the novel a sense of reality. Any similarity in other names, characters, places, and incidents are entirely coincidental

Chapter 1

Nadia

Waking up to my phone constantly ringing, I rolled over on my side to look at the time. It was six in the morning, and I knew that I wasn't going back to sleep after this. Only one person would blow my phone up back-to-back the way this person was. Doing a quick stretch in the bed before I picked up the phone, I tried to do whatever to give her a chance to hang up the phone but knowing her, that wasn't going to happen. Not even looking at the phone, I slid the green icon on my iPhone to answer my best friend.

"Why the fuck are you up this early, Jayda, and secondly, why the hell did you decide to wake me up with you?" I asked her irritably.

No hello or anything. I wanted to get straight to the point. I knew what today was. I should've known that this call was going to come from her sooner than later. She knew I hated today with a passion; yet, she still did everything in her heart to try to make it the best one for me. That was one of the traits I loved and hated about her.

"Because my best friend finna, she finna… go best friend, that's my best friend," Jayda sang into my phone.

"Jayda, why are you blowing up my phone so fucking early with this foolishness, knowing I don't get up for work until another hour?" I asked her back, unfazed.

"Well, fuck you too, Nadia. Grumpy hoe. Are you on your period today with the nasty attitude you have?"

I'm pretty sure she thought she would have broken me by now, but I knew if I gave in like I wanted to, she would plan things for us and take this way overboard. I didn't think I was ready for that just yet.

"I know you don't usually do anything for your birthday, friend, but you deserve to be spoiled this weekend. Your parents would want this for you. You're young, you don't have any kids, you don't have any fucking plans, so pack your bags before you head to work. Our plane leaves tonight for Vegas. I'm not taking no for an answer. I'm going to make sure this is a weekend you won't forget!" She screamed into my phone before she hurriedly hung up. Jayda knew what she was doing hanging up before I could give her an answer.

I hung up the phone and laid my head back on the pillow to think about what Jayda said. She was right. I was almost thirty with no kids and no love life. You could put me in the category of a nun if you wanted to. It was that bad with me.

I would talk to Jayda when I made it to the daycare. She wasn't only my best friend since I'd met her in college, but she was also one of the teachers at the daycare I owned, Chosen Ones, here in Vicksburg, Mississippi.

Me and Jayda had been through so much together. She was my roommate in college all four years at Jackson State University. We were both going for our degree in Early Childhood Education, and we both loved kids. The only difference in our career path was she wanted to become a teacher, and I wanted to own my own daycare.

Jayda was going beyond an Early Childhood certificate, just in case she wanted to move up and do more. She had the love and passion to have her own daycare soon, and I believed my friend would be perfect. I would never think of her as competition. I was always the friend cheering on another friend no matter what. If a person didn't cheer me on during anything I accomplished, I didn't need that type of person or bad energy around me.

Being with and around kids melted my heart. I was an only child who had lost my parents on my eighteenth birthday — which was why I still hated to celebrate to this day. How could I celebrate a day that caused me so much hurt?

My parents were everything to me. Being my daddy's only child and girl had its perks. My mother made sure I had everything, but there was just something about being a daddy's girl that I couldn't get over. They made sure I had everything my heart desired. There wasn't a time I could remember that I didn't have what I asked for. My mother and father both worked at a factory overnight, so they would've come in the house the morning of my birthday before I had to go to school — or so I thought.

I couldn't forget that day if someone paid me to. It was seven years later, and I could still remember the details of that day like it was yesterday. On the morning of April 30, 2015, my eighteenth birthday, a woman officer came to my home, knocking on our door. Thinking it was my mother and father, I ran to the door, expecting them with balloons and gifts like any other year, but that wasn't the case.

Going to the door, call it paranoia or whatever you wanted to, but I could tell from the way she knocked on the door that it wasn't my parents. I don't know if I was just used to my parents having a certain knock or what, but I knew it wasn't them. For some reason, on my birthday, my parents and I had a thing where they knocked on the door as strangers, looking for the birthday girl with gifts. I loved the goofiness of my parents, and we kept that tradition going on every birthday I had. It was like I could still hear them, like they were there with me.

"Hello, I'm looking for a birthday girl who requested a Baby Alive doll," my dad spoke from the door as my mother smiled beside him on my fifth birthday

I jumped up and down with so much excitement as my pigtails swung back and forth. My dad could tell from my excitement that I loved that moment. Now, I cherished every moment and every birthday that we shared.

The way the person banged on the door wasn't a knock I was used to. I looked out the peephole of our front door to see who it was. I was eighteen and legal to be at home alone, so after looking through the peephole, I opened the door for the officer.

"Hello, are you the daughter of Olivia and Jayson Burlington?" she questioned. I shook my head yes as she continued to talk to me.

"I'm sorry to inform you that your parents were in a bad car wreck leaving work, and they didn't make it. If there's anything else you need to know, you can call down to the station to let them know your next step. They're going to need you to come to the morgue to identify your parents' bodies also. Again, I'm sorry for your loss," she informed before backing away from the steps with a sorrowful look on her face.

Shaking my head up and down again, I slowly closed our door and slid down the wall. Not a thing could be heard in my home but my sniffles as the tears dropped from my eyes. At eighteen, I knew nothing about planning funerals. My mother and father weren't big on being around their families, so I didn't know who to call on. After about an hour of crying on the floor, I knew it was time for me to put my big girl pants on and see about my mother and father.

Walking up the steps to their room, I went into the closet to get the big yellow envelope they made me never forget about. They always told me if anything happened to any one of them, the instructions of what to do were left in this envelope that I thought would be used further down the line.

Tears escaped my eyes effortlessly. It was like I couldn't stop them. As much as I was trying to be an adult in this situation, I just couldn't do it. Was this really happening to me? I was parentless in a matter of hours. Calling the number on the envelope and asking for Mrs. Betty, I told her everything that was written down on the paper for me to say. After I finished the call with her, she informed me that I didn't need to head to the morgue; she would handle it. In my head, I was screaming thank you because I knew that would've been one of the hardest things I'd ever have to do in my life.

A week had gone by, and I had finally gone to the funeral home to pick up my parents' ashes. Mrs. Betty had informed me that my parents requested to be cremated, and there was really nothing I could do about it. My emotions were starting to get the best of me. I never even got the chance to show them all the acceptance letters I'd received from the schools we sat down and applied to. Many nights, I would stay up, trying to write all those schools and fill out my applications to not choose any one of them.

I had chosen to stay close to home since I wasn't used to anywhere else, and I'd accepted the offer to Jackson State University. The house we stayed in and the 2009 Toyota Camry my mother and father had bought me last year were paid for, so the money from their life insurance policy would go towards my future and making them proud.

Within the first month at Jackson State University, I met Jayda and we clicked instantly. I thought my roommate would be someone the total opposite of me, but that wasn't the case with Jayda. She was laid back and wasn't a nasty female. One year later, our friendship became a little deeper, and Jayda let me know she stayed in and out of foster homes and had lost her parents early in her life too, just in a totally different way from me.

We had been through so many obstacles, trying to obtain this degree so after four years and graduating college, I decided to invite her back to my hometown with me. I still hadn't touched most of the money from my parents' life insurance policy. The good thing that came from it all was I was accepted for FAFSA and didn't have to pay a dime of my money for school. I stayed on campus, but I still went home from time to time to make sure everything was okay with the house.

My home was only about an hour and a half away from the school, but the hurt of going there just wouldn't allow me to stay. The year I graduated was the year I decided to move back into our home. Jayda not really having family and the bond we made with each other, I brought her back from school with me. Not even six months later after coming back home I had found a house that was on a major street and turned it into my dream daycare. I'd had my eye on this property since my last year of college. I was happy to see it was still there and at a better price than what I saw it for. At the time I looked it up, I knew it was going to be a lot of work to change it into what I had pictured in my head, but with the ideas I had swarming, I knew I could bring it to life.

Jayda wanted to find a job to help me with the bills at my parents' home, but I had to turn all her advances down and let her know all I needed from her was her help and support with the daycare. We painted the rooms in the daycare and found different things for the classrooms. Within three months, I had my daycare up and running. Jayda even made the curriculum for each of the teachers to have for their children in the classroom. That was all the help I needed from my friend. The only bills I had were the light bill and the water bill at the house and since it was just us, the bills didn't cost me that much money there. She wanted to work for free, but I turned that down also. There was no way I was going to give her that. She was working just like any other teacher I had in my daycare.

My parents had a three-bedroom home, so I kept my room and let Jayda get the guest room. Only thing to do at my parents' home when I came back was to buy new furniture for the living room. I always kept my parents' room door closed; nothing had been moved in it.

I still sometimes went into their room to lay under their covers. It made me feel close to them. The way their scent still lingered spooked me at times because it was years later.

After about two years when things were up and running and money started flowing with the daycare, Jayda found her an apartment. There was no love lost. I understood that every grown person needed their own space.

Snapping from my thoughts, I didn't want to keep thinking about the memories that got me here because I knew it would be a harder day than it already was. No matter how many years went by, I yearned for my parents. To see their faces and how proud of me they would have been to see me bringing my dreams to reality. That would have been everything to me.

Every year after work on the anniversary of their death and my birthday, I would go to their graves with flowers and memories. This year would be no different. My birthday was just a day to me that I no longer chose to celebrate. I knew eventually, I would deal with things better, but I still couldn't tell you when that would be.

Finally, after being up an hour in my thoughts, I threw the covers from around me and got out of my king size bed. Walking to my walk-in closet, I went to look for something to wear. It was Friday, our last workday of the week. I let everyone dress in casual clothes on Friday. I grabbed a white shirt that had the daycare name and logo on it, a pair of True Religion jeans, and my undergarments from Savage Fenty out of my drawer and got in the shower.

I grabbed my Dove sensitive skin body wash and poured it onto my bath sponge. I rubbed the sponge against my body as the hot water ran from the shower. This was something I needed to relieve the stress from my body. A hot shower always did that for me.

After about forty-five minutes, I felt refreshed stepping out of the shower. I got dressed before doing my hair because I knew if I did that after, it wouldn't look the same. I pulled my scarf from my head, and my thirty-inch bundles fell down my back the minute I freed it from under. I took the pin curls down from the night before as I refreshed my baby hairs in the mirror. I grabbed my Marc Jacobs perfume to spray on and my all-white Jordan 12's out of the closet. I was a sneaker fanatic. Yes, I wore my heels during the week but the minute I left the daycare, they were off.

I wanted to get a full look at myself. I walked to my full body mirror, spinning around in a circle. I had to admit, I was a boss and most definitely a baddie. I looked way better than the way I was feeling, and that was my goal. My brown, caramel skin was flawless. Standing at five-foot-seven, I had thirty-six Double D breasts that belonged to me. My waist was snatched, thanks to the gym and my waist trainer I wore half of the day. I didn't have a big ass, but it was enough to get a nigga's attention if need be. My hair was natural and went to my mid-back, but you wouldn't know because all I wore were wigs or braids, so I didn't have to maintain it.

I thought about what Jayda had said earlier, and I went back into the closet and grabbed my suitcase from the top shelf. This birthday would be different from the others. It was time for me to smile for my parents instead of crying and being miserable on their day and mine.

I knew the weather was always hot in Vegas, so I decided on a couple of two-piece outfits, sundresses, and a couple of club fits. I knew who I was going with. I had to be prepared for anything with Jayda; and like any other woman, I packed enough outfits to last a month, and we were only going for the weekend.

I could hear a familiar ringtone on my phone that I hadn't heard in a minute, but he always made sure that every year, he told me happy birthday.

Greg

Happy Birthday Na. I hope you enjoy it. Call me if you need anything.

After I read Greg's message, I threw my phone down and continued packing. It seemed crazy that after all these years out of college, I'd never changed Greg's ringtone from "Separated" by Avant. I had been through many phones, but I still seemed to put that ringtone under his name. I guess I was kidding myself. I still wasn't over the hurt he'd done to me, and that was my petty way of still dealing with it. It was true; the minute I finally let go of him, I couldn't stand him. He caught me my freshman year with him already being a junior at Jackson State. Who was I to know that I was running into the biggest hoe on the campus? I didn't have a sibling or my mother to steer me away or give me game about the older boys at the college.

So here I was, fresh in, believing everything that he told me. He could have told me we were going to get married and have kids by the time we got out of college, and I would have believed him. That's how dumb minded I was about him.

The parties started to roll around, and the different girls posting pictures and making statuses about him continued. I knew I loved him, but I loved me more. Not a thing had changed with him over the years. He was now married and still trying to get with me every chance he got. I hadn't been in a real relationship since the hurt from that one.

Greg would always be my first love, but I just wished he would understand that we would never be anything more than friends, no matter what happened or changed in our lives. Men always remembered the one woman that got away, and I knew by the text, he knew that too.

Chapter 2

Jayda

I was online, searching the web to get my best friend the fuck out of Vicksburg this weekend for her birthday. I understood and truly knew how she felt about her parents. No, I didn't lose mine the same or have them that long, but I did feel that same void of not having them around.

Nadia had been a Godsend for me since the first day she'd come into our dorm room. She helped and pushed me to continue on nights that I just wanted to drop out of school and never come back. I would never forget. Nadia had a big heart and would give you her all if it meant helping you through whatever you were going through.

There were many nights I felt like I didn't belong with everyone else at the school, but I had worked my ass off to get there. Some things I'd done to get where I needed to be I wasn't proud of, but it was too late to give myself a pity party now. The things I had to do to survive I would take to my grave before I came out of my mouth to tell anyone, even Nadia. I loved my girl, but I didn't have the nice life she had before she got here. I had to grind and get it out of the mud to get through my life.

I even knew it would sneak back around and bite me in my ass, but the damage was already done. If anyone found out what I did to get here and pay my tuition, nobody would look at me the same — not even Nadia and she didn't judge anyone. She had become my best friend but not even she knew those big secrets that I held from everyone.

No one even knew where I was from, only that I had come from Jackson State University with Nadia. Not one person ever questioned me about my life before meeting her, and I let it stay that way. The more I kept that old life behind me, the better off I would be. If I brought that me back to the surface, I would dig up things that were supposed to die the minute I left that lifestyle alone. I was no longer that person. As much as I wanted to revisit things and people, I couldn't, and I was the only one to blame for that.

I knew that everything you did in the dark would come back to light and that all dogs had their day. It would only be a matter of time before it came back on me, and I just prayed I could dodge that bullet for as long as I could, or that Nadia never got hurt on my behalf.

I grew up in foster home to foster home. I never stayed in one place too long because I would curse out all the parents they gave me or let the ladies know about their pedophile ass husbands. No woman seemed to want to know the truth; they just wanted the check — never to make sure that I was truly taken care of.

No matter where I stayed, though, I always went to school every day. That was like my safe haven away from everybody and everything that I had to go through. I guess that was one thing I could feel good about. My foster parents never sent me to school with dirty clothes on for people to talk about. Once the kids knew I was a foster child, the jokes came.

I never really had friends in school. I stuck to what I knew —which was my work. My last year in junior high school, I got really close to my teacher, Mrs. Carpenter. I told her about wanting to become a teacher and leading other students. She didn't laugh at me or talk about me like my foster parents would. She took me under her wing and taught me as much as I could take in.

As I grew up, I learned and understood how I wanted to start young and educate the younger generation on how important things were in life. If you started early, letting them know the importance of school and education, maybe they would take it more seriously down the line. Even though I knew when a person had their mind made up, nothing we did or said would change their feelings. That's why I chose to stay away from the older students, from grades six to twelve grade. I didn't want to deal with it. At that age, they got to feeling themselves, and I just didn't have that much strength in me. If that was the case, I would've chosen to be a counselor.

Hearing my phone ringing, I looked down to see a blocked call calling. I picked up the phone to see who the hell could be calling me from a blocked number. I held the phone to my ear to see if the person would say anything while they thought I wasn't on the phone. I heard no one on the other line, though. Not even a background noise.

I finally spoke into the phone. "Hello?" Still, no one responded. I said hello about five more times before hanging up. I knew damn well nobody was playing on my fucking phone this early in the day.

I knew I had just broken up with my ex-boyfriend, Keith, about a year ago. I figured that one of his hoes had gotten a hold to his phone and seen all those begging ass text messages the nigga was leaving. You could do a lot to me, but the outside kids were when you had to go. I could take a lot of things, but that just wasn't acceptable. Once you crossed that line, there was no coming back from it.

He still wouldn't tell me to this day who his baby mama was, and I was beginning to think the hoe was ugly or something the way the nigga was hiding her. I knew eventually, we would run into each other. This town we lived in was just too small not to.

Men these days — well, boys these days — wouldn't know when they had a good thing on their side, even if it jumped up and slapped them in the face. My light complexion gave people the idea that I was mixed with black and white; and to be honest, I truly didn't know. I knew my mother was black, but I had no clue who or what my father was. Most people thought I lost both of my parents. In reality, I just said I lost both so they wouldn't question me further.

My mother was a well-known crackhead where we were from. She was known to do anything she could for a high except one thing — giving them me. I was off limits to anyone in exchange for drugs. Luckily my mother did have some morals when it came to me. The new and upcoming drug dealers who served her weren't into things like touching younger girls, and I was thankful she hadn't run across one yet.

There were many times that some of our family would allow us to stay but after a day, my mother would steal something of theirs, and we would be homeless again. I knew she stole those things they implied, and I was only a little girl. Our relatives would get tired of her running the streets and in different crack houses with me and offer us their home for a night. They would ask me anytime they saw me if someone had touched me, but I was blessed to say that hadn't happened to me. As much as they claimed they felt sorry for me, no one ever asked her to leave me behind.

To this day, I still don't know who ended up telling on my mother, or if it was just a coincidence, but out of my sleep one night, I was lifted into the arms of an officer. I looked around the abandoned building, and my mother was nowhere in sight. I didn't even put up a fight with the officer when he carried me out of the nasty house. I didn't know whether she ran when they came, or if she was out getting high. All I knew was that I had been left alone in the world, and that feeling followed me through life forever. I wasn't that small, little girl anymore, though. I was a grown woman who had made a way for myself.

I had freckles on my cheeks, giving me the girl next door look with my sandy brown hair. I loved when I wore my hair curly in its natural state. I was on the smaller side. I had small, B cup breasts and a small butt. My pretty face made up for all of that, though.

That was one thing I was glad of. I didn't have low self-esteem. Everybody around me was either plus size or had a little meat on their bones in school. Skinny girls weren't really in style, but that never stopped me. I walked like I had a donk behind me, and nobody could tell me different.

I had gone into a little daze, thinking about my life. That was only the half, and I didn't want to think about that anymore. I woke up early this morning because I knew it would take me a minute to choose the exact place that would show us a good time. My friend, Aliza, wanted to come also, but Nadia just didn't fuck with her, and I didn't want to mess up my girl trip. I was shocked that she didn't say no to me. She just hadn't had the chance to let the hurt go from her parents, and I could understand that.

Nadia was a people person but at the same time, she wasn't. She would handle people well professionally but personally; she didn't trust people easily. She felt like Aliza was a backstabber in the making and gave her an off vibe. I was Aliza's daughter's teacher, and we just started to vibe after dropping her daughter off every day. Nadia and that damn vibe she always picked up on was the reason it was still just me and her to this day. Whatever she chose, I would stand behind her a hundred percent, but I was okay with having other friends. I was a little less cautious I guess you could say. I would party with whoever until they did something wrong to me. Nadia didn't give people a chance to cross her, and I also understood that also.

Nadia was so overprotective of me, and I loved it and hated it at the same time. I wasn't a baby. I could make my own choices but at the same time, I knew she meant no harm.

I finally came across two tickets to Las Vegas. We were both in need of a weekend, and the saying *what happens in Vegas stays in Vegas* was about to come true for us. I had so many things planned for us to do to keep our minds from the daily things we both had going on in our lives.

I knew the minute I walked into the classroom and saw my baby's faces, I would feel a lot better. Oh, how I wish I could've made better decisions that would've allowed things to be different for me. But for right now, I would just cherish the eight hours I had with my little babies at the daycare.

Ever since Keith and I had broken up, I had been staying away from men and their lies. I missed the hell out of him, but I also knew my worth. I'd just started getting back to myself and learning me all over. I couldn't lose that again.

I tapped *book* on the screen of my computer to confirm our trip. I knew this was about to be a weekend that neither Nadia nor I would forget.

Chapter 3

Champ

Stirring in bed, I looked over into my beautiful fiancée's face. A nigga couldn't believe that on Sunday, I would tie the fucking not in Vegas. Yes, I, Champ Hoodman, was about to be off the market. I had been off the market for a minute now but like every nigga around, I fucked up from time to time.

When you owned a bar in downtown Atlanta, you had a lot of women throwing ass at you just to get a job; and some of the hoes threw the pussy just to keep it. I was a nigga, so of course I fell for temptation a few times when I shouldn't have.

I was a thirty-one-year-old chocolate male. I stood at six foot one with a perfect set of white teeth at the top with a bottom row full of gold clips I could take on and off. My body was ripped with tattoos all the way up to my neck.

I felt like I was at the age where games and shit were over with. I no longer had time to argue with three or four bitches a day. A nigga like me really wasn't about to be taking care of a woman who didn't truly belong to me. I wanted peace and a family now.

I switched things up in the bar and even hired a manager to be more hands on with the girls I had working here. The less temptation I had to deal with, the more I lived a peaceful life. What was that saying? A happy wife was a happy life. All the arguments didn't seem to be worth that headache to me. A quick nut could put you in lifetime situations, and I really didn't need or want that. I wasn't on that type of time. The woman who bore my child would be my wife.

Only thing I could offer them was a job at the club to make them money. Me paying for pussy was something a nigga like me could never do. That shit was against my morals. Ain't that the shit the females said nowadays? Women gave that to me just off the strength of me being me.

Just my looks alone made the women drop to their knees, ready to suck me off without even asking. It was word of mouth around here that kept me in trouble. The minute they heard the story about a nigga's dick game, they wanted to try it out. I didn't have to offer to pay a bitch with shit but these nine inches of thick meat. That was the problem; they knew what they were getting themselves into but never knew how to stay in their place.

In the back of their mind, they would swear it was something more they could do to make me leave the one woman I loved, never realizing that she wasn't the fucked up one; it was just my choice. We grew up a little slower than the women, so we brought them more problems than they could bargain for at times. My girl had thick skin because I knew for a fact the stuff I put her through, I couldn't stomach if she did.

Those women were only bitches and hoes to me, but the one laying in my bed was my queen; she had a nigga's heart. She had been here with me since I didn't have much to my name but a dream of what I wanted.

After my father's death, I had closed myself off from a lot of people — even her and my mother. She never stopped doing her womanly duties or got in her feelings about my late-night drinks at the club. That was when my cheating got worse. I just didn't give a damn. I felt like my world had been tampered with, and I had to figure out a way to deal with it. I won't sit here and act like I was right, but I was in pain and hurt people, hurt people.

She stayed down through the cheating and never changed. Yes, she left a nigga for a while, and that time apart showed me that I couldn't live without her. There wasn't a woman alive out here bad enough to fuck that up for me.

I had to Keith Sweat, beg, and plead to get her back home, but a nigga had to do what the fuck I had to do. I would take that shit to the grave because if Sean heard what I did, that nigga would never let me live it down.

I heard my phone vibrating on the dresser next to me, so I slipped out the bed so I wouldn't wake her. I grabbed my phone and walked towards our bedroom door.

"'Sup, nigga?" I answered Sean.

"Are you sure this what you wanna do, nigga? Leaving me to be alone in this hoe shit when we started this shit together," he cackled.

I laughed into the phone. "Glad I didn't have your ass on speaker phone because I wouldn't be able to hear the end of that shit had I been. That's why Kira don't like your ass now."

"Mane, you know I'm with whatever you want, but something not right about her ass. I'm telling you, man, but out of respect for you, my boy, I will be the first one there beside you. But you know I can't let you go out like that. Get your shit ready, do whatever ass kissing you have to do to little Mrs. Sneaky. I'm taking your ass to have a bachelor party tomorrow. The plane leaves tonight."

"Man, I told Kira I wouldn't have one of those — especially if your ass was throwing it. You know how the fuck those end up turning out. You gone have me waiting at the alter in my white tux, looking like a sad puppy because some shit done got back to her," I told him, rubbing the back of my head because I knew what I was saying was true, but I also knew he wasn't listening. I peeped my head over to the bed to make sure that Kira was still asleep. I knew I couldn't tell her about this.

"What the hell is going to happen at a bachelor party with just me and you? You need to have her bachelorette party recorded because all her friends are hoes, and I'm telling you, birds of a feather flock together, my nigga," he informed me.

"I will see you tonight for this shit, but I'm telling you now, I don't want none of that shit you have planned," I told Sean knowingly, as I hung up the phone.

I'd hung up the phone and headed to the bathroom to hop in the shower when I realized that Kira wasn't asleep on the bed anymore. As I neared the closet to grab my clothes, I could've sworn I heard a nigga say something back to her on the phone, or maybe I was tripping.

"I promise, I'm going to handle it," she said to someone on the phone.

Backing away from the closet, the shit that Sean said started to stick with me. Did birds of a feather flock together? Did she take a nigga back, only to play me in the end?

She said she would be leaving out tomorrow for Las Vegas and we were headed out tonight, but that was something I didn't plan to tell her. I'd planned on ditching Sean with the hoes and going to surprise my girl there.

All a nigga wanted to do was gamble and enjoy myself with my girl. We had come too far to let anything, or anyone, push us back. So, I would brush that little conversation off because maybe I was thinking some crazy shit right now. Walking out the closet, Kira bumped right into me and jumped.

"Fuck, Champ! I didn't know you were right there. You scared the hell out of me," she told me, fidgeting with her hands.

"Kira, you know damn well can't nobody get in this

muthafucka unless we let them in. I make sure security is tight around here for you. Don't ever doubt that you're not a nigga's first priority," I spoke, staring straight at her.

Looking at her face, I couldn't read her expression. She stood on her tiptoes and kissed my lips before walking back to get in the bed. I couldn't lie. Kira's beautiful, golden-brown skin and those doe, brown eyes got me every time. She always took care of herself and kept herself up, even in the house. Sometimes I just wished she would allow herself to be comfortable in our home.

She didn't have to be on her trophy wife at all moments. I wanted to see her hair all over her head or her in her sweats sometimes — in her natural state.

Something just wasn't right with her after that phone call but eventually, she would let me know. What she didn't realize is, I knew her like a book and her body language was giving me bad vibes. Hopping in the shower, I decided to go into the office today and make sure that everything was together with the club before I left.

Chapter 4

Sean

I hung up the phone with Champ and had to light the fucking blunt just to calm my nerves. That was my brother from another mother, and I loved that nigga to death, but that bitch Kira just wasn't right.

How do you go from mad, leaving this nigga's house, to telling him she wanted to get married all in one breath? Like, you just fucking went from I hope you fucking die to till death do us part.

I was about to call around and check to make sure she hadn't put any life insurance on my brother or worse — voodoo. If she knew like I knew, she would keep it the fuck moving. I would have her ass dead before she could even cash the fucking check.

I called to let him know I was taking him to a bachelor party and the whole time, we were going to catch this bitch in whatever she had planned. I looked at all her friends' pages, and not one of them got an invitation to a bridal party, and none of them were saying their favorite ass female line, *What happens in Vegas stays in Vegas*.

I knew Champ had done some fucked up shit. Hell, he was a nigga. We all had at a point in time, but you could tell when a woman came back for get back or to get her nigga back. Nobody in this world could tell me any different. She wanted to get even, and I was here to end all the shit before it started.

If I was wrong, then hell, a nigga could admit his wrongs. I would even pay for the fucked-up ass wedding. Who the fuck you know want people hanging from the fucking top of the roof for a wedding? A little dramatic I would say. The shit on TV is meant to stay the fuck on TV. Tyler Perry had really fucked these women up with that.

I cruised a few streets. I had to hit a couple of my houses to make sure that everything would flow well while I was gone. I knew it would, but I just had to take extra precautions, or these niggas would become sloppy.

I paid nicely to make sure the police weren't something I had to worry about. Wherever you went, there was always a person you could persuade to do things for money. Money was the route to all evil and in this situation, I appreciated it. I'd been running the southside of Atlanta for a couple of years now without my name ringing bells. The only way you'd know who I was, was if you were one of my top soldiers and still, I could've just been the middleman. They never knew.

I stayed in my own lane, and I minded my own fucking business. If I had a problem, I ended that shit before it could even fucking begin.

Pulling up to Porsha's crib, I knew this pick up would go smoothly. She had more heart than a lot of these niggas I knew around here. If I mixed business with pleasure, I would give her every inch of this curved dick every single day, but I didn't, so that one time would have to be that one time.

I was a bachelor, so I was really chillin' and exploring my options. Being five foot eight and a hundred and seventy pounds, I kept myself toned in the gym. Having waves that would make you seasick with my million-dollar smile, I had many choices. My brown skin didn't have a tattoo on it. My teeth were pearly white like I had gotten veneers. Keeping my hygiene up was something a nigga like me would never slack with.

I parked my Tahoe on the street and chirped it before heading to the door. I looked around, checking my surroundings before I walked up to the door. You never knew who could be following you or watching you. I knew about that all too well. I didn't give a fuck who I was, someone was always looking for a come up, and I'd hate to be the one to make a statement to keep your hand off of things that didn't belong to you. I stepped into the house as Porsha moved to the side to allow me in.

Before I could even get to the door, I heard the knobs turning. That was another thing I liked. She was always aware of her surroundings. She stayed in the hood but one look at the inside of her apartment, it was nothing like the outside.

Her furniture was spotless due to her not having kids. Nothing was on the floor or out of place, and I could smell the food coming from the kitchen. You couldn't have thought a nigga like me would eat any and everybody's cooking, but Porsha could throw down.

The way she whipped my dope, I should've known her skills went beyond that. Heading towards the couch, I fell back to get a little shut eye for a minute. I hadn't had any fucking rest since this morning, trying to get the stuff situated this weekend for me and my Champ.

No lie, Porsha knew I wanted her, and I knew she wanted me, but she wanted her money more and I had to respect that. Every time I came for my pick up, she had my money and a plate ready for me to eat.

She walked by me with all that ass hanging out of her pink shorts, knowing I would slap her on the ass. "Porsha, take your ass on. You already know what it is, but a nigga do got eyes," I told her honestly.

"I'm ready when you are, Sean. You keep playing games and

lose a real bitch to one of these other niggas if you want to. I won't wait too much longer for you, stink," she spoke before getting up to get my plate and the bag I came for.

"Porsha, if that's what you want to do, love, don't let me stop you. I told you, ma, I can always find another person to do what you do, but I can't mix business with pleasure again."

See, that was my problem. I knew she was a gem and didn't want a nigga to reap the benefits. I knew sooner or later, I would have to respect her space — or at least try to. Threatening her bought me a little time.

"Iight. Say less, my nigga," she told me back with an attitude.

That's the shit I hated with Porsha. She would turn her nigga mode on quick like shit didn't faze her. That was my fault for fucking her that one time I came to pick my shit up from her, but I couldn't help it.

She always knew what the fuck to wear. I didn't know if her ass was watching the window and would run and put the shit I liked on or not. That night, I walked through the door, and she had my food, blunt, and pussy waiting on me. What more could I ask for?

I knew the minute I put a title on things, things would change. Once Porsha got in her feelings about me not being what she wanted me to be or not coming when she wanted, I knew that would affect our business relationship and about my money and dope, I would have to hurt Porsha. I wouldn't want to, but I would definitely make arrangements.

"Let me get the fuck out of here because I can tell by your attitude you done transformed from Porsha to Pusha P on a nigga," I told her jokingly.

Seeing her smile made my day. I leaned over to give her a kiss on the forehead and got ready to head out. I knew me and

Porsha would be the true definition of fucking toxic and the line of business I was in, I couldn't have that. Taking one last look at her ass in her shorts, I headed back out, making sure to lock the door behind me.

She didn't understand she wasn't the nigga, and she didn't run shit. Gathering the rest of my pickups, I decided to head to the house and catch a nap before our flight. I was going to be on my Inspector Gadget mode the minute we landed, and I needed to be rested. I just had this feeling things were about to hit the fan.

Chapter 5

Nadia

I changed my mind. Not wanting to start my day with all the sympathy and sad faces, I decided to shoot Jayda a message to let her know to check in with the teachers throughout the day and make sure that everything was going to run smoothly. I sent her that message with no worries whatsoever.

I knew, without a doubt, Jayda could run that place with her eyes closed without me being there. She had built everything from the beginning with me. I just wanted to start my day off celebrating with my parents before I caught the flight to Las Vegas. I knew she probably thought I had changed my mind, but I would text her once I left the cemetery to let her know that everything was still a go.

About thirty minutes later, I was pulling up to the cemetery, not even giving myself time to pull up in front of my parents' graves. The tears started falling down my face instantly. Closing my eyes and exhaling, I continued listening to "I'll Be Missing You" on the radio of my car. I leaned my head back and closed my eyes as I took in every word that Faith Evans sang.

Every step I take, every move I make
Every single day, every time I pray
I'll be missing you

Thinking of the day when you went away
What a life to take what a bond to break
I'll be missing you

Listening to those lyrics took all of the pain I was feeling away at the moment because that was exactly how I felt. The bond that was broken was irreplaceable for me. No matter how much I pretended to be okay, I just wasn't.

I opened the door to the car slowly as I got out with the flowers. I had gotten them the night before. Sitting in the middle of the ground so I could be at both of their graves, I rubbed my hands across their tombstones. As my eyes got blurry, reading their names, Olivia and Jayson Burlington, on their tombstones, it still felt unreal.

This place was a place I hated because when I came here, it was like a slap to my face, knowing that they were never coming back. Yes, I knew that they were gone, but when I was away from here, it felt like a dream that I hadn't awakened from. This place made me face reality, and I hated it; that was why I rarely visited them. It wasn't that I didn't want to; it was just easier to mourn them away from the cemetery.

"I promise, I miss y'all so much. If tears could bring y'all back, y'all would have been here by now. I know y'all are both proud of me, and this isn't how you'd want me to be, so this year, I'm living for y'all, I promise," I expressed to my parents as I kissed their graves one by one. I got up to get everything, including the information I needed for us to leave tonight. It was time for me to make my parents proud and stop all this sadness for them.

"To be absent from the body is to be present with the Lord. The righteous man who dies is taken away from evil, he enters into peace." My lips trembled as I mumbled the scripture to myself. I had to realize they were in a better place, but the selfish daughter in me felt like I needed them more than God did.

Pulling away from the grave site, I decided to stop at the store by the house to get us some snacks and other things to have while me and Jayda waited to board the plane. I headed into the

Kangaroo gas station and pulled up to the pump to fill up to get that out of the way for when we came back Sunday.

Moving things around in my purse, I was trying to find my Bank of America card so I could pay for the gas. I peeped my head up to look at my surroundings to make sure no one had walked up on me. We lived in a crazy world nowadays; you could never be too safe.

My eyes landed dead on Keith. I could've sworn I knew the car that Keith was getting out of but nowadays, everybody had the new Honda that came out. Not too many had that smokey colored gray, though. I tried as hard as I could to hop out of the car to catch the license plate before they pulled off, but I couldn't.

"Shitt!"

Yes, my girl said she was done with him for the moment, but she always doubled back with him, so I was just trying to be protective of her. Seeing him kiss the person and get out of the car didn't bother me at all. It was the fact that I knew I'd seen the car that he got out of before. When our eyes met, it was like he'd seen a ghost. There was something about the nervous look he gave off, like he'd been caught. That made my best friend instincts tingle.

Now that the vehicle was gone, I began to walk into the store. I guess Keith still had to get something out of the store because I could see him from the side, jogging, trying to catch up to me.

"'Sup, Nadia, how you been?" he asked me.

"I been good, Keith, how about you and the baby?" I had to throw that out there to let him know that I knew everything that happened with him and my girl, and I didn't fuck with him like that.

Holding his hand up in surrender, he backed up. "I was just speaking. Good to see you, Nadia, and tell Jayda I said she could answer a nigga calls and texts."

"So, you want me to tell my best friend, after you just finished kissing someone in that car that you got out of, to hit you up? You crazy as hell, Keith. I'm just saying, she could do better," I told him, shrugging him off.

I went to the opposite side of him. I grabbed our favorites and headed to the register to check out before leaving the store. Keith had lost his mind. There was no way in hell that I was going to even bring his name up to my friend.

She was in a happy place now, and I wanted her to stay there. At times, I wanted to ask her if she missed her hometown because I brought her here and not one time did she ever talk about going back. I knew she was in and out of foster care, but she had to have someone she missed. Right?

Knowing how sensitive I was over my family, I decided to not bring that up right now. This weekend wasn't about bringing up anything in the past; it was for us to escape it. I would just ask her another time. It wasn't like she was hiding anything from me.

Chapter 6

Champ

No lie. After talking with Sean and seeing Kira acting nervous after that phone call, I couldn't shake that feeling after I left the house. It was like a nagging little devil on my shoulder saying, "dawg, she playing you", and I couldn't get him to go away.

Right now, I had bigger issues going on at the club, so that would have to wait. But I was going to figure out what and who had her in her feelings. She'd just better pray that it was some friend shit instead of anything else.

Kira would regret the day she ever came back into a nigga like me. Yes, I did what I did before we got back together, but I'd been doing right by her. All this pussy being thrown at me in the club, and I still hadn't let temptation win. Even the girls I had working here noticed it. All of them would walk by and say I was on some new me shit. I didn't even sweat it because I was. Nothing was wrong with manning up and being with one woman. Any female who acted like you were crazy for doing it was never going to be wifey type.

Clicking around on the computer, I made sure that all of our inventory was to my standards for the weekend and that VIP had everything it needed. Now, I just needed to know one thing. Why the fuck were my numbers off? If I wasn't anything, I was a man who knew numbers. Never had my club had the deposit come up different than what it was supposed to.

After clearing through all of my paperwork and speaking

to my staff and manager, almost three hours had gone by. I laid back in my chair, looking up at the ceiling. I didn't know whether they were good actors, but I believed everything my dancers and manager said. I didn't think either of them could've taken the money out of the deposit bag.

I took the deposit bag out one more time to count it to make sure I hadn't miscounted. I knew there was no way I miscounted almost ten thousand dollars but again, I was a thorough guy, and I wanted to check behind myself again.

KNOCK! KNOCK!

Hearing the knock at the door, I never stopped my count before letting them know they could enter.

"Come in," I told them, looking up to see who was walking in.

"Hey, boss. Can I talk to you for a minute?" Christianna asked me as she tucked her hair behind her ear and took a seat.

She sat, bouncing her knee like she was nervous about something. I knew damn well Christianna wasn't about to sit up here and tell me she stole my shit. I wouldn't give a damn if she was trying to save the universe. There would be no exemption to me sending her ass to jail. Her three kids were about to be touching their mother's hand from prison. She had been my only manager I allowed to be the last person to touch the money because she'd proved she was trustworthy.

Once everyone paid out for the night and all of the registers were counted down, she was the last person to see and count the money before it was placed in the bag. The bag was never sealed because I did the final count before I dropped it off to the bank that morning.

Christianna had placed way more money than this into the deposit bags within the past year, so why was this time any different? I placed the money down to give her my full attention because I felt like she was ready to talk by the way she stared dead on, looking directly at me, rubbing her palms together.

"Does what you want to talk to me about have anything to do with this money in front of me?"
I questioned her as she looked down at the money and then back at me, shaking her head up and down.

"Why would you take from me, Christianna? You could've asked me for anything, and I would've helped you," I told her honestly. You could hear the disappointment in my voice, like I was scolding my child in front of me.

Jumping up from her seat, she looked at me with a blank look on her face like she was confused.

"Fuck you mean? Why would I take it? I didn't say no shit like that. Excuse my language, but I love my kids too much to leave them behind taking some money. I'm not making millions here, but you pay me enough to make sure I'm able to take care of my family," she told me, damn near yelling the first part.

I was going to let her make it because I did speak on her without giving her a chance to say what she had to say.

"So, what is it about this situation that you want to talk about?" I asked again, sitting back, looking her dead in her eyes because I was confused, and I didn't like that one bit. If she knew something, she needed to open her fucking mouth and get it out already. I just wanted to get down to the bottom of who the fuck touched my money. No, my bar wasn't going to close over ten thousand missing, but it was the principle about it.

"Well, I did see someone come into your office the night I sat the money on your desk. I knew only me and you had a key, so I thought the money was safe, placing it back on your desk," she told me. I guess she could feel my frustration by the look on my face, telling her to get to the fucking point.

"Who came into my office, Christianna? That's the only other answer or word I want to come out your damn mouth next."

"Well, umm. I'm not saying she took it or anything, but I know I didn't. Kira came into the office that night and said you left something and asked me to open your office. I didn't think anything of it because hell, she's about to be your wife," she told me, almost like she was scared to keep going.

I nodded my head, letting her know that she could leave. I decided not to even alert Kira of me having a bachelor party or even going to Las Vegas tonight, so I didn't pack shit. I'd made up my mind that once we landed in Vegas, I would get whatever I needed.

It was always hot out there, and a nigga was really ready for this vacation. Maybe it was what I needed. Lately, I'd been feeling stressed. I didn't know if it was because I was finally getting ready to say I do, or that I just really didn't want to go along with it anymore.

This wedding was only because Kira wanted it and what Kira wanted, she got from me. It seemed like she was getting whatever she wanted, even when I wasn't the one giving it to her. She couldn't have known that the money was going to be on my table. Why didn't she call me to let me know she was taking anything? Maybe she just wanted to get something for the wedding, and she didn't want me to know about it.

I hoped some things would change after I gave her this wedding. I'd done some things, but I apologized, and she took me back, so I never wanted to hear about the situation again. Once you forgave a person, the only time you brought things back up was if you never truly forgave them. I was hoping that never became a problem for me and her.

I loved my fiancée, but I refused to be miserable or be asked about the same shit over and over. She had a right to side eye a nigga because actions spoke louder than words but lately, I was doing just that. I'd get home before a certain time so she wouldn't think I was with bitches, and I surprised her with different gifts on the bed almost every morning. To me, it was the little things that counted but sometimes, she acted like her heart wasn't in it anymore.

I wasn't the type of nigga who had to sweat, beg, or make anyone do anything. I just hoped we could make it like it was. If not, she couldn't say I didn't try.

I had been at the office for hours, hearing my phone ring. I knew it was almost time to get the fuck out of ATL.

"What's up, nigga?" I answered as I picked up my phone.

"Nothing much. Everything's settled on my end; I was making sure you hadn't backed out on a nigga. Ole save me the last dance looking ass nigga," he told me, laughing.

"Man, I was waiting for you to hit me up. I'm going to leave the club and head to the plane. I was just gone buy my shit when I got there or have something delivered from the store.

"Cool. I'm just finishing up my shit I got going, and I can meet you within the next hour there," Sean instructed before hanging up.

I hung up with Sean and looked down at my watch. That would put us leaving at about ten-thirty, so I was cool with that. It would take us about four and a half hours to get there, and that was perfect timing to get off and hit the casino.

I knew that I had a longer drive than him, so I decided to go ahead and head to the strip that we were leaving from. No, we weren't niggas who couldn't get on planes with everybody else, but I just liked to be alone and, in my head, when I was in the sky.

Me and Sean had the money, so why not from time to time buy dumb shit? Sean hit me up one day, asking if I wanted to buy a plane with him. I knew he was gone get it with or without me, so I didn't miss out on the chance. We went that day and paid for the plane in cash. We had a person who was always on standby for whenever we needed the plane to go.

Charles was an older guy, good dude, but when we got in the air, I didn't give a fuck who he was. Before we pulled off, I would google shit to ask so that nigga checked to make sure this shit never went down. He would laugh at me, but you could never be too safe nowadays.

You never knew when an enemy was lurking or when your past would come back for you. I hit one big lick with Sean. I didn't ask him any questions. I was already flunking out of college after losing my father. I had completely stopped going. That lick had us set to do things we couldn't before. I always knew my heart was never into that type of lifestyle, so after that one lick, I walked away, but Sean decided to stay in it. Once he gave me my share from that night, I got what I needed, and I opened my bar. Sean respected it.

Pulling up to the strip at the same time as Sean, we slapped hands and boarded the plane. For some reason, I knew this would be a trip that I would never forget. The thing was, I didn't know if that was a good thing or a bad thing.

Chapter 7

Nadia

We were finally getting off the plane and landing in Las Vegas, Nevada. The whole plane ride, I stared out the window and continued to have pep talks with myself. I was doing the right thing, and I knew it. I wanted to be in my home, cuddled under my covers with a bowl of ice cream and the other part of me wanted to be the drunkest person in the room in Las Vegas. It was too late now to back out; our plane was landing. I could tell we'd reached our destination when I started feeling the bumping that happens when the landing gear came out.

"Ladies and Gentlemen, Southwest welcomes you to Las Vegas. The local time is 10:00 p.m. For the safety of those around you, please remain seated with your seat belt fastened and keep the aisle clear until we land," the flight attendant told us over the speaker.

I reached over to wake Jayda up. You would've thought she was in her damn bed the way her mouth was hanging open.

"Jayda, get up." I mushed her head, trying to wake her.

She stirred a little bit before she opened her eyes. You would think she didn't know where she was. She stretched a little and looked around.

"We're here?" She asked me like she didn't see all the damn lights had been turned on.

I was glad I was on the outside because I was about to leave her on this plane by her damn self. I stood up to retrieve my carry-on from the bin right above our seats. Jayda had understood the assignment because she was now up and on her feet. I knew Jayda, so I was pretty sure she had gotten us a rental. She would want to go every damn where and sightsee, and she hated being on someone else's time.

"Friend, I'm so fucking glad you decided to come out here for your birthday," she expressed, sounding more excited than me.

"In a way, I am too. We both needed to get away. We've been through a lot and tonight, we let loose," I told her, turning around to do a little twerk for her.

"I know the clubs are open until two a.m. here, but I would rather wash up and gamble tonight. Tomorrow, we can begin to prowl and see what Vegas has to offer," I told Jayda, hoping she gave in to me.

I shook my head as I laughed at her side eyeing me, but I really did just want to chill tonight. I loved cards, so tonight I was going to try my luck at the blackjack table. It was still my birthday, and I was hoping to have some luck. Going to grab our bags, we walked to where we had to get the rental from.

Everything was so close here, and lights were everywhere. It took us about fifteen minutes to get to MGM Resorts. I was glad she got us somewhere to stay that had a casino connected to it. Since we were staying here, parking was free. We found a spot that wasn't too far from the elevator and headed to our room. Jayda was lazy, so I knew she'd already checked us in from her phone. It had only taken her a second to run over to the front desk to grab the cards to get in our room.

While she was doing that, I walked around and checked out the hotel with my mouth wide open. Trust me, I was used to nice things, but my best friend had gone all out for me. I didn't think anything could get better than the hotel until she handed the room key to me to open the door once we headed to the room. I walked into a decorated room with balloons everywhere. There was even champagne sitting on the bed. Turning around with tears in my eyes, I couldn't be so thankful for a friend like her. Jayda had really gone beyond my expectations, and she didn't know how much I appreciated her for it.

"Happy birthday again, bihh, 'cause my best friend finna... go, best friend, that's my best friend, that's my best friend," she sang to me again.

This time, I joined her in the turn up. Turning around to twerk for her, I was starting to feel good about today, and this hadn't happened to me in years. It had been a while since I felt like this day was my birthday and not the day that I'd lost my parents.

I unlocked my phone and scrolled through it to get to my Snapchat app to capture this moment. I rarely used it, but this was one of those times where I wanted to show off my happiness. I took a picture and a small video of the room, captioning it *fuck your best friend. Mine is better* and tagged Jayda in it.

I knew her other friend, Aliza, would see it, and that was what I wanted. I hated her sneaky ass, and I knew soon, the truth would come to the light about her. I didn't know what, but I knew something about her just didn't sit right with me. I just hoped Jayda didn't get hurt in the end.

Looking around, I realized the room only had one bed. I slowly looked over to where Jayda was to see if she had lost her damn mind. I loved her, but we were too damn old and had enough money to where we could get a double bed or two rooms.

"J, you my friend and all, but I'm not with this one bed shit. You might get drunk and decide you want to try some new shit, and I'ma have to beat your ass," I told her jokingly, but I was dead ass serious.

Falling out laughing, J was tickled, but I didn't see a damn thing funny with this shit. If you walked in, you would want to congratulate the couple on my birthday, the way this shit looked.

"Friend, you're fine and all and if I swung that way, you could most definitely catch this pussy; but that, I'm not. I don't know about you, but I plan on putting this pussy on a real nigga down here and going back home with a smile on my face."

"Now you know me fucking on a random nigga isn't going to happen, Jayda. I don't think there's a person clever enough to get me to do that here," I informed her.

"Touché, friend, we shall see. I'm right next door to you, though, so let's get freshened up and hit the casino," she told me as she headed to the door to go to her room.

I peeped my head out of the door to make sure she got into her room. I didn't like not sharing rooms because we were so far away from home, but she also knew I would curse her ass out if I turned over and her ass was fucking in the bed beside me. I closed my room door to freshen up. Hopefully, I'd win some money tonight.

Later that night

I went over to knock on Jayda's door so she could hurry her ass up. She came out, dressed to kill like I expected her to.

I promise, you would think that my friend was mixed with something from that natural curly afro, those freckles, and her pretty skin.

She had on an all-black romper that fitted her small frame, all black Jordan ones, and a pair of black Jordan socks. I guess you could tell we wanted to be comfortable because I promise, I had close to the same thing on.

"Okay friend, let me find out you're taking them booty enhancement pills the way you starting to poke out a little," I told my friend, giving her my sign of approval, even though she didn't need it.

I had on a short romper set that was all black with spaghetti straps and a long blue jean jacket shirt, Nike socks, and a pair of red and black Jordan 12s. Like I said, I was a tennis shoes girl, and we were not about to be gambling in heels. You could surely dress down and still kill a woman who was half dressed with all of their skin showing.

This simple stuff we had on was sure to still turn heads. Men only wanted one thing nowadays, and it had nothing to do with if you had a tight dress on or a choir dress. To them, pussy had no face.

We walked to the elevator and got on. My eyes landed right on the guy who was already on the elevator. I thought God came down and sculpted this man himself. You could tell the cologne he wore was expensive. It was giving him nigga with money vibes. His dreads were twisted neatly, and oh my God, the edge up was so crisp, you could tell that he had to have just gotten his hair tapered. His pearly white teeth showed as he smiled at us when we walked in. My flood gates opened instantly. I damn near wanted to touch below and make sure I didn't have a wet spot. The Balmain jeans that were slightly hanging off him gave him an edge.

I could see Jayda's ass trying to get my attention, but I wouldn't be giving her any eye contact until this man was off of this elevator.

I had an instant attraction to him, and that usually didn't happen to me. Usually, I wasn't interested in most men who were interested in me.

The hairs on the back of my neck stood up when I felt him moving from behind me. Jayda pressed the button for us to go to the bottom floor, and I didn't even notice that another button was pressed.

Moving out of his way so he could get off, all I could do was stare at this man. Not even paying attention that he was staring back at me, he smiled.

"If you're going to stare, baby girl, you might as well ask me my name."

I snapped out of the daze I was in. "I wasn't interested, so I didn't think to ask," I informed him.

He laughed to himself as he got off on his floor. The doors closed, and I could finally breathe.

"Bihh, did you catch that fine ass man? And yes, it was the dreads for me. All I need is one night and just a few minutes, and I'ma handle that there, and then I'm through with it." She sang "Like That" by Webbie as we laughed together. I had to give it to him. He had me wanting to know more about him.

"Jayda, he got on here and I'm telling you, I had to hold my damn breath not to scream. That man had done something to me, and he didn't even have to open his mouth. I'm for sure staying away from him. He has the ability to make me go back on my word about putting this fat ma on somebody I don't know down here. I can tell now, he would fuck up more than just my mind."

Shaking my head, me and Jayda headed out of the elevator to the main floor and for some reason, the guy was still embedded in my mind.

Chapter 8

Champ

Walking straight into the room, I knew Sean was gone clown me for this, but I just had to let him know what had just happened to me in the elevator. I felt like a young nigga in high school, scared to talk to his crush.

"See, I'm telling you, shit like that is temptation I don't need," I told Sean as I entered our suite.

"I don't even want to ask what happened, Mr. Meet Me at the Altar in my White Tux looking ass. I know you're not about to mention anything about another woman who isn't Kira," Sean's annoying ass blurted out.

This was why I hated telling this nigga shit.

Ignoring his little funny joke, I walked over to sit on the couch to finish smoking the blunt before going downstairs to gamble for the rest of tonight. I just didn't feel like doing anything besides chilling tonight.

I had to give it to her. The way she snapped at a nigga had me ready to hem her ass up right in the elevator. Something about her just made me want to grab her and kiss that attitude right out of her, and that wasn't something an engaged man should want to do.

Looking over at Sean, I could tell he thought this shit was hilarious.

"Maybe it's faith with y'all. The Lord sent the woman I'd been begging for to remind you that you were about to make a mistake. They say he might not come when you need him, but he's always on time. You never know what might happen this weekend," he said to me like he wasn't over there playing while speaking on God.

Looking at his ass skeptically like he knew something I didn't, I just shook it off. There was no need in me telling him anything about what he'd just said because then, he would say some shit that was even dumber.

I wasn't trying to think about nothing right now but winning some damn money. Baby girl was beautiful. Maybe in another time we could've been something but right now, I was good, and I was about to marry a woman I loved and had taken through hell. She deserved that from me.

We walked on the elevator and headed down to the blackjack table. I was ready to try my luck. I walked closer to the table. I could tell that the girl from the elevator was sitting down. The way that her hips were exposed in her romper and the way she sat so comfortably dressed down made me wish Kira was a little more like her.

I pulled the chair that was beside her. I could smell her Blossom by Gucci perfume. Her laid-back attire had a nigga in awe because most females wouldn't have come down here like that. I shook my head to myself. I had to make a cross under the table. This girl beside me was Satan to me because she had me wanting to do things that I knew were off limits. It was cool to think certain things as long as I didn't act on them. I had this shit under control. I coached myself.

I looked up from the table for a minute. I had a feeling that somebody was watching me, or maybe I was just bugging because I was around a lot of people in an unfamiliar location.

I could've sworn as the doors of the elevator closed that Kira was on the fucking elevator. I knew her from anywhere. Even if it was just her back turned to me. I knew her that well to know that it was her. I knew I'd had too many drinks because she wasn't supposed to make it until tomorrow. I told Sean that mixing that clear and brown on the flight was a bad idea.

After a while, I realized I was just playing to keep baby girl beside me company. Since we were the only two at the table, I didn't know if it was the curiosity or the feeling of this liquor that made me start asking her questions.

"What brings you to Vegas, if you don't mind me asking?" I asked her. I could see her side eyeing me, deciding if she wanted to answer.

"Today is my birthday and my friend decided to treat me to a trip for the weekend. Usually, my birthdays are not the best, but this year is turning out to be a little better," she told me with a small hint of sadness in her tone.

"Today is your birthday? Happy birthday, beautiful, and I wish you many more. Let me get this next drink and whatever else you're having for the rest of the night on me."

Turning to the side, she smiled at me and took her umpteenth shot and put her glass back down. I could tell she was tipsy already and needed to get back up to her room. Hell, I was too, and I hadn't drunk drank nearly as much as she did.

"Let me get you back up to your room. I wouldn't want anything to happen to you once I left; it'd really fuck me up," I told her honestly.

"Aww, you'd care if something happened to little ole me? You don't even know me," she giggled, further letting me know that she was drunk.

"Yes, the girl was good as drunk," I spoke more to myself.

"What floor is your room on? Where is your homegirl?" I asked her while helping her out of her chair to walk towards the elevator. I knew there was no way she was out here, tore up, alone.

"Floor sixteen," she said as her eyes opened and closed.

Even drunk, this woman was beautiful to me. I couldn't help but check her out from head to toe. Hitting floor sixteen in the elevator, it didn't take us long to make it to her floor since we were the only two on the elevator. We walked off. I could tell she was lifting her arm, telling me to take a right; her room was right there.

"Do you have your room key on you?" I asked her.

I didn't even see where she had reached to get her key card. Taking the key out of her hand, I walked her in the room. You could tell today was her birthday. She had balloons everywhere. The balloon numbers had twenty-five written out, and there was a bottle of champagne on her bed that she hadn't even opened yet.

I laid her across the bed, and the minute her body touched the mattress, she grabbed ahold of my neck. Looking into each other's eyes, it was like we were meant for each other. My soul was calling out to her as hers to me. Just as I was about to remove her arms from around me, she kissed me. I knew that I shouldn't have, but I kissed her back. Even though the shit was so wrong, it felt so right. I promise, after this, a nigga was done; I was going to take this to the fucking grave. I had no self-control whatsoever.

"Are you sure this is what you want?" I asked her. Shaking her head up and down, she motioned that she was. That was all the confirmation I needed from her. I was about to give her one hell of a birthday gift. One I didn't think either of us was going to forget.

Pulling the spaghetti straps off, I slid her romper down her body. Baby girl was a damn freak because she had nothing on under it. I laid her body down. I wanted to take this slow with her. I went to pinch her nipples as I went down her stomach, kissing all parts of her body till I got to a place I'd been thinking about since I saw her in the elevator.

"Oooohhh!" she let out as I continued to kiss and suck all over her body. For some reason, I didn't wanna just fuck her; I wanted to do the thing I had no business. Make love. I knew this was a one-time situation, and I wanted to make the best of it.

Latching my tongue on to her pearl, I held her thighs in place. Sucking gently and sticking my finger into her pussy one at a time had her trying to squirm out of my hold.

"Let that shit go when you're ready, ma," I instructed her.

The way she started rubbing on a nigga's head while I was eating her pussy had turned me into a demon. The shit sent me into overdrive, feasting on her. I could feel her legs begin to shake. I knew she was close to reaching her peak, pulling away before she could. She popped her head up.

"Why did you stop?" she said, almost like she was begging for this to continue.

"Nawl, you have to ask for this dick before I give it to you. Now tell me you want this dick, and your wish is my command," I told her, being her genie for tonight.

"I want it, please give it to me!" she begged. The way she begged for the dick made my dick harder than what it already was. That was exactly what I wanted to hear before I went into her sweet spot.

I had to adjust myself for a minute because although sad to say, this was the best pussy I'd ever had. The way her muscles squeezed my dick, I would be coming in no time. I had to take control of the situation. I gave her long, slow strokes to fuck with her mind. Then, I began to fuck her nice and hard while sucking on her breasts, one by one.

"Fuck baby, right there! Don't stop! Right there!" she screamed out.

Hearing her talking to a nigga, I knew from there I was on the verge of coming right along with her. Getting into the same rhythm as her, I started fucking her roughly while she threw her ass back against my dick, putting my hand around her neck, making her look at me dead in my eyes.

As we stared into each other's eyes, I knew then I was fucked. I would think about her and this session forever.

"Fuck, I'm coming," she gasped.

"Let it go, ma. I'm coming with you."

Letting out a loud grunt, I let my load off inside of her, not thinking anything of it.

We laid there for about ten minutes before either one of us moved. I finally got up to get a towel and cleaned us up. Watching her on the bed, her body was laid out. I didn't know if she had gone to sleep, or if she just didn't want to say anything. While cleaning her, neither of us said a word. There was so much that needed to be said, but neither one of us could say it.

Knowing I should have taken my ass back to my room, I laid down in the bed and allowed her to doze off into a deeper slumber. Waiting till she was fully asleep, I slipped out of the bed to head to my room. I knew it wasn't right, but what was I supposed to do? I kissed her forehead, pulled the money out of my pocket, and sat it on the dresser as I headed out. I had fucked up.

Chapter 9

Jayda

I had been watching Nadia and that fine man from the elevator all night. I see why my friend had a look in her eyes like she wanted to devour him where he stood in the elevator. It had been a while since Nadia took someone seriously. She had mingled with a few men, but it never went past the talking stage. I was a proud friend, watching her from afar.

My friend loved to gamble and mess with anything dealing with cards whether it was blackjack, pitty pat, or spades, all you had to do was pull out cards, and she was coming. Me being more of a slot girl, the minute we headed off the elevator, we both agreed to meet back here in a few hours.

Nadia gambled like a man shooting dice, so I knew we would be here till early morning. She never thought I would get far enough away from her to where somebody would snatch her up, though. We were in a whole 'nother state. I couldn't leave her out here, blind. A predator could've been out there, lurking for a woman who was by herself.

I know people probably thought I was talking crazy, but the things that went on in today's world, you shouldn't count anything out. I wanted to have an eventful weekend, but not so eventful to where I didn't come back with my best friend.

I was happy my girl was letting her guard down and even talking to him because if he knew like I knew, he was a lucky man. My friend was beautiful and had a good heart. All she needed was somebody real to share it with. She was the type that once she got hurt, she said fuck love. As much as she loved me, not even I could convince her differently.

Steady tapping the machine, I was losing all of my money, but I guess you could say in a way, that's what we came to Las Vegas for. I knew I was going to lose big or win big.

"Fuck," I thought I had mumbled to myself.

"These machines are getting me too, baby girl, it's not just you," a guy from beside me mentioned to me as he looked over from the machine that was beside me.

Before acknowledging him, I had to do a quick peep view to check out his appearance. There was a certain criteria you had to meet for me to even give you a conversation. I wasn't stuck up or anything, but I had a right to be picky about the person I gave my time to.

I started with the shoes. They had to be clean. They didn't have to be name brand, but that could give them bonus points with me. The teeth had to be straight, and his cologne had to match his face. I hated walking past a man who smelled good and the minute he turned around, he looked like an ugly duckling.

I took him in from head to toe. He was very easy on the eyes. My eyes went from his feet all the way to his perfect white teeth. The way they were neatly lined up, I wanted to know if they were veneers. Those are very popular now. The gold cross chain he wore around his neck to the Gucci belt he had around his waist caught my attention. Even the sweet-smelling Creed cologne that was coming off of his body made me want to savor it. This man was indeed fine, and I couldn't resist letting him walk off before shooting my shot. I hadn't been touched by a man in over a year. He didn't know it, but he was about to be my next victim.

I turned sideways so my body could face him while he looked at me without a care in the world. When a nigga knew he was that damn fine, it was a bad thing. Not one time did he put me on blast for checking him out. It was obvious I was checking him out, but he didn't care, which let me know he was very confident in himself, and that turned me on.

"Now that you're finished checking me out, can I have your name?" he told me, snapping me out of the little fantasy I had going in my head, thinking about the things we could do together. I had already seen Nadia go upstairs with the guy from earlier. I knew my friend had drinks, but if she needed me or if push came to shove, she would scream before she allowed something to happen. So, I decided to shoot my shot at the gentlemen in front of me.

"I'm not for the gambling and I'm not from here, but I do have something on my list I'd like to check off tonight," I told him, being straight forward while I smiled at him devilishly.

Not saying a word, he looked at me, putting his fingers under his chin.

"No, you don't want to know my name or nothing? You just want to use a guy like me, huh? Are you naughty or are you nice? Since you're checking off your list, I need to know because I feel like you're trying to use me," he jokingly questioned me.

"My name is Jayda, and I'm a little nice and a little naughty; it just depends on the situation. I've told you my name, so what's yours?" I finally asked him, trying to get past the greeting phase.

"I'm Sean and no, I'm not interested in what you have planned tonight. I don't move like that. Be safe, lil' mama," he told me as he walked away, leaving me flabbergasted.

I turned around, back to the machine. I was so ashamed, I knew my hairs were standing up on the back of my neck. I wasn't going to lie. I was actually shocked about what the fuck just happened. I wasn't an ugly female, and I rarely got turned down. I guess I just wasn't his type. I shrugged the situation off.

Moments later, I could feel someone tapping me on my shoulder. Really not in the mood, I was about to turn around and go off, but I could smell his cologne before I even turned around. Turning around slowly, it was the same guy from a second ago, Sean.

"I'm just messing with you. You should've seen your face, baby girl. I watched you from the machines over there, and the pitiful look on your face dragged me back over here. Let me buy you a drink or something first before we get our night started," he said while still snickering about the situation.

I could only look up and laugh because he did have me in my damn feelings. I was really about to pick through myself to see what the hell could have gone wrong. He had me questioning if I had something in my teeth or if my breath smelled like liquor. Any little reason to figure out why he had dismissed me.

"I guess I'm going to call you Kevin Hart Junior for the night since you're a funny guy and all," I told him as I turned to head to the bar.

"We can just wait for a beverage server to come by, and I'll grab you whatever you like, but I can't leave this spot. Sit with me and I'll fill you in since you're my company for the weekend," he told me like he knew I would knowingly agree to that.

I looked at him out the corner of my eyes while I waited on a beverage server to walk past. "I said tonight; I didn't say the weekend."

"Take it or leave it. Since I don't do this blind date stuff you got me on, you have to give me your weekend."

I shrugged my shoulders, giving in to his little demand. He looked like he could show me a good time this weekend. I just hoped I could figure out a way to spend time with Nadia and enjoy this weekend with the guy in front of me. I didn't want to miss out on this opportunity of spending time with a man who could make me laugh. I hadn't had this in a while, and I knew deep down, I needed this.

"Why can't we leave this spot? You here spying on your girl or something?" I asked him, needing to know the full run down.

These days, men didn't care, so hell, I just had to ask to make sure I wasn't putting myself into a messy situation. Anything could happen at any given time with what he was on. He could've been watching to kidnap or rob a person, and I was sitting there, playing, like I was his Bonnie. Nawl, I wasn't going for that. Right plan, wrong person.

"I'm telling you now, if anybody comes looking for your ass on some bullshit, I'm not the rider type of girl that people pretend to be now. I'm telling on you expeditiously."

"Nawl, I'm not on that type of time. I got a feeling that I'm going to bump into someone who's not supposed to be here, and this is the only place I can see the front entrance and the elevator."

"So, like I said, you're spying on someone," I told him, throwing my hand in the air to be more dramatic.

"It's complicated," he expressed to me, thinking I was about to end this conversation.

"Well, let's make it uncomplicated." Looking to my left, I could see a woman bartender a few machines down.

Waving my hand in the air, trying to get her attention, she strolled over as she finished with getting the man's order before us.

"Hello. What can I get you today?" she asked me.

"I will take a frozen strawberry daiquiri and for him a…" I looked over to him, waiting for him to finish off his drink order for her.

"A Corona in the bottle for me," he told her, placing a twenty on her tray and turning back around to tap on the machine.

I guess him turning around confirmed to her to keep the tip as she walked off to get the orders she'd written down in her section.

"You need to wait to take a sip of your beer, or are you ready to give me this tea?" I asked him like I was talking to one of the girls.

"J, take that girly ass talk elsewhere. It's really simple. I'm trying to catch my best friend's fiancée cheating," he said clearly, like nothing was wrong with any of this.

"How do you know that he wants to know she's cheating? Some things are better left for them to find out. You can be friends with a person for years, but when it comes to your significant other, they outweigh the friendships every time," I told him, speaking from experience.

"You're speaking on this situation like you know more than what you're telling. You could be right, but the man in me won't allow my friend to get played by anyone. If it comes down to us losing friendship behind it, I can respect my decision and his," he told me while taking a sip of the beer the waitress had given him.

I was so much into my own head, I didn't even realize that the bartender had already placed my daiquiri on the machine in front of me and handed Sean his beer.

"Enough about me and why I'm doing what I'm doing. Where are you from? Tell me a little bit about yourself," he questioned me like everything was okay, but I could tell by the look in his eyes, he was still thinking about the words I had just spoken.

He was waiting on me to tell him about me, but that wasn't something I was ready to talk to anyone about. That would make me open old wounds and bring back memories I wanted to stay buried. I didn't know who all he knew and where he was from. One little slip up could cost me my life.

The conversation between us had died down. We now had an awkward moment that I hated I started. I had to open up my big mouth. He was still sitting where he was, looking directly at the door and elevator. I just wondered what he would do and what would happen if she actually walked through that door with someone who wasn't his best friend and how it would end once he told him.

Chapter 10

Sean

I walked Jayda to her room to make sure she made it safely before I went back to my spot downstairs. I was glad to see nobody had sat at the machine I was at because I was destined to get my money back from that machine.

While walking Jayda to her room, I could see her from the side of me as she walked, taking slow steps behind. I hadn't been around this woman but for a few hours, and it was like I could read her already. She was wondering what she could've done wrong to make me want to bring her back to her room. I could tell she was ready to go up to her room because she had stopped playing and was only watching me tap at my machine for about an hour. The slight yawns she tried to hide were also a dead giveaway.

No words were being said between us, and I didn't want her to sit here with me all night, knowing that the result still wouldn't be what she wanted. I had to figure this shit out with Kira before it was too late, no matter what the result would turn out to be once everything came out in the open. I just couldn't give up on my plan. She tried the best she could to get me to stay, but I had all weekend for that. I wasn't a nigga who was pressed for pussy, and I could tell how beautiful she was that she wasn't in need of a man. I would make it up to her. If nothing came through for me within the next few hours, I would give up on looking for Kira.

I knew Kira liked the finer things and this was one of the best hotels out here. It was only a matter of time before she came out of one of those elevators or stumbled through the lobby. Maybe I was just trying to find something wrong in her that wasn't there. In my head, there was no way you could dog me out and I didn't get some get back. Once I had upped the score, maybe everything could go back to normal. Just maybe.

Jayda's words started popping back up into my head. Would he really choose her over me? I sounded like a bitch asking myself that. I knew the answer, though, but it was still on my mind. I had to put myself in his position. If my girl, who I'd put through hell, came back into my life, and my friend had information to show me she wasn't genuine, I wouldn't want to see it. I'd want to live my shit as perfect as I possibly could. It would have me wondering why the fuck were you looking into my girl without my permission anyway?

Things were going well with them. Who was I to stand in the way of another person and their happiness? I could see me now, telling him some hard evidence and he stayed. Wasting my damn time. I would clown his ass so bad, he wouldn't have a choice but to cut me off.

I was over this shit for the night. If I saw her, I saw her. If I didn't, I didn't. I flagged the waitress down to get me another beer. I had one more in me before I decided to take it in for the night. I continued tapping on the machine in front of me. It was past three in the morning, and I was still down here, losing my fucking money. I wasn't moving until I won at least half of my money back. This machine had my money, and I felt like they had robbed a nigga. Until I got my shit back, I was going to sit here comfortably.

That was just the gambler in me. Even though I knew I should've been getting my ass up before I lost everything in my pocket. I really didn't know how much I had lost. I was just steady pulling bills out of my pockets. I continued to pull until nothing came out of it. I had to shake my head at myself. Losing this money didn't put a dent in my pocket at all but damn, I could've spent this shit on some shoes or something.

I leaned back, hearing a loud commotion behind me. I could tell that it had to be a bunch of drunk ass dudes probably here for the same reasons we were. There it was, that little person in my head, telling me to turn my head. If I would've turned around any moment later, I would have missed her.

I looked back to catch Kira going into the elevator just in time. The problem wasn't that she was going into the elevator. The real fucking problem was who she was going into it with. It had been a long time since I'd seen his ass, but how the fuck could Kira know him? I wouldn't forget his face if it was the last one left on this earth.

At first, I thought this was just her on some cheating shit, but seeing her with him let me know this shit was bigger than I thought, and it was time for me to start planning. A fucking storm was brewing, and I hated to tell Champ about this, but I had no other choice but to fill him in. I knew that sneaky bitch wasn't shit, but I never thought she would have stooped that low.

Chapter 11

Nadia

I lifted my head up in bed. Not even giving myself a chance to lift up completely, I let my head fall right back down. I felt like a ton of bricks was holding my head down the way it was thumping. I knew I couldn't handle liquor like that. I had no reason throwing them shots back-to-back like I was a big dog and in reality, I was a little puppy when it came to liquor. I was thankful for being prepared because I had put a box of BC Powder in the dresser drawer beside the bed.

I sat up again, trying my best not to let the vomit that wanted to come up get there.

"What the fuck is this?" I asked myself, looking at the money sitting on the dresser. Did his ass think I was a prostitute or some shit? Sliding the drawer open and getting the box of BC out of the dresser like I originally planned, I slammed it back shut. This man had me so fucked up, it was a shame. I looked up to see that the hotel water bottle they left in the room when I first came was still sitting beside the card, welcoming me to their hotel.

I didn't even care about the sickness that I was overcoming every step that I took. I needed to get this BC in my system so I could get to the bottom of whatever this was that he called himself doing. When I took a BC Powder, I knew it would work within the next thirty minutes. Twisting the top of the water bottle and pulling the paper off the top of the BC, I poured it into my mouth. Drinking a bit of water, I frowned. Even though the powder worked fast, the taste would never get better. Within the next thirty minutes, I would be back to myself, or halfway there at least. I just had to lay back and let the BC do its job.

I closed my eyes, only to be taken over by the memories of last night flashing before me. The way he caressed my body and took me to a height I had never gone to before. That man had me calling him all types of shit, and I didn't even know him. I bit down on my bottom lip. The way it felt reminiscing was like he was still here in the room with me. My body was turning warm all over, and I could still feel him giving me slow strokes. The way we stared at each other last night, I had to turn my head from him because of how intense our stares were at one another.

I was giving this man all of me like we grew up together and hadn't seen each other in years. I didn't know what had come over me when I shook my head, agreeing for him to have my body, but I couldn't deny the feeling of amazement that he gave me. Having sex on the first night was not something I had ever done before. I had every right to feel like a little slut bucket because he slutted me out in the most respectful way I had ever seen.

I popped my eyes back open, only to look over again and see the money still laid on the dresser. Last night meant something to me, but it obviously didn't mean a thing to him. Who in their right mind would think it's okay to leave money on a dresser after a sexual exchange and think it's okay? This nigga outright paid me like I was a fucking prostitute. I didn't know if it was his guilt consuming him or what. Now that I think about it, the man could have had five baby mamas, a delusional ex-girlfriend, or a whole wife at home, and I didn't care one bit. It was truly too late to think about that now, but I still couldn't help but wonder.

. Enough time had passed, and I could feel my headache leaving. Now it was a little better to stand up and walk. I looked around the room, trying to see where I had put my cell phone. I was hoping I didn't lose it or leave it at the blackjack table.

I finally found my iPhone 14 Pro Max over by the bed. I picked it up, knowing that this wasn't the place I'd left it in. I scrolled through my messages, seeing that Jayda wrote me a few questions, asking if I was okay and that she had made it up to her room. I had every intention of filling her in about this eventful night of mine. She wasn't a judgmental friend; she was more of the friend who was about to cheer me on for the shit I had done. She wanted me to go out and find someone for me but the way our generation was built, men didn't have a loyal bone in their bodies. I was built on loyalty and respect, and neither were being given. Morals were something a lot of women lacked, and respect for women was a thing that most men lacked. Men thought they were the prizes in a relationship, and I just wasn't with that.

Bestie Jayda
HURRY UP AND COME OVER SO I CAN TELL YOU ABOUT LAST NIGHT!!

I sent Jayda a text, hoping she would've read the message and come over by the time I'd gotten out of the shower. She was all for juicy gossip, so I knew if she hadn't shown up or responded, she was still asleep. She was a late sleeper, but I knew that couldn't have been something she planned on doing during this trip. If she hadn't responded to my text or called me back, I was going to trade places with her ass and become the annoying friend. I needed to wipe all of these sins off of me that I had created last night before I began my day.

I made my way to the bathroom after gathering everything I needed from out of my suitcase to head to the shower. After about an hour, I was out of the shower and dressed. The white onesie tank top and the light wash blue jeans shorts I had with my khaki wedge heels had me giving pretty girl vibes. It was still my birthday weekend, and I was ready to see what the next two days would have to offer me. Walking out of the room, I felt an emotion I hadn't felt from myself in a long time — happiness!

Bang! Bang! Bang!

You would have thought I was the hotel manager coming to tell a person that they were over the checkout time the way I was beating on Jayda's room door. Usually, I was the one dragging my feet to start our day. I hated to be around people for a long time if I didn't have to be, but today, I wanted to get out and get some air.

As I was about to make my last ghetto knock, I could hear her taking her main lock off the door as I stood there, waiting with my arms folded together.

"Damn, took you long enough. You had me waiting outside the door like I was a Jehovah's Witness, asking for your time," I told her, brushing straight past her as she stood behind the door to hold it open.

I looked around the room, checking under the bed and opening the bathroom door, trying to make sure she wasn't in here hiding anybody. How long she took to open the door, I was hoping I found somebody. Jayda was a hard sleeper, but her ass didn't sleep that hard.

"Nadia, why do you have to be so damn dramatic all of the time?" she expressed, walking back to the bed.

"Because I wanted to change places and be you today. Who put a stick up your ass? This is supposed to be a fun weekend for the both of us. You're sitting here being Debbie the downer," I spoke back to her, flopping down on her bed.

"Why the hell are you so happy? Nothing is wrong with me. I'll be ready in an hour to start your day off and get this tea from you. I saw you leave with the man from in the elevator," she told me, brushing off the question I'd just asked her.

"GIRLLLLLLLLLLLLL," was all I could seem to get out. I was still mad about the money he left on the dresser, but I decided to throw it in my purse and charge that little night to the game. The way he left, I knew there was no need to go find him. He showed me exactly how he felt about me. I couldn't blame anybody but myself because I put myself out there for him to do that.

I knew Jayda was going to take a minute, so I opened my phone to my Facebook app and went through my messages. I saw Aliza had liked our photo. I clicked on her page to see if she'd written a slick status, and she did exactly what I thought she was going to do. I knew I had no right going to look at what was on her page, but oh well.

Aliza headbitchincharge Love
You can tell I'm a great friend. I don't mind lending my biffy to anybody for the weekend.

I clicked off of her page because for one, the bitch was too old to have that shit in her name. That was the shit we did in high school. Like always, everybody was liking it and loving it, but I saw straight past her bullshit. Before I could click off, I saw she had one comment. Clicking on it to be nosey for the last time, I saw Jayda had commented with the cross finger and blowing kiss emoji.

I wasn't jealous by a long shot but once again, I could see Jayda falling for the bullshit like Aliza was innocent. She wrote it right after I posted my video, but nobody thought that was awkward. I was pretty sure they did, but nobody called her out on her bullshit. I didn't want to ruin my day, so I grabbed my things and walked right out of Jayda's room. She could call Aliza and talk about that friendship. Call it petty, but I hated when she played that damn slow role. I looked down at my feet, and a pedicure was needed. I decided to take time to relax and lose this attitude I had gotten.

Chapter 12

Kira

"Let me get this right. This nigga done took you through hell and high water, and you're still ready to marry him?" He fussed at me, walking back and forth from the bedroom to the living room area I had in my hotel suite. I could tell by the way the vein in the front of his forehead stuck out that he was pissed with me. But oh well, he just didn't understand, and my decision wasn't meant for him to.

"Well, everybody deserves second chances. You should be the main one to understand that. I've done my dirt as you know, and he's done his dirt. Two wrongs don't make a right, Mike," I expressed to him, trying to answer his question as simply as I could. I really didn't know if I meant what I was telling him, but it sounded good at the moment. I could tell by his little head nod as he walked back to the couch, he wasn't feeling the way I responded.

He really had me rethinking my whole life with Champ. Could I really let go and forget about all the hurtful things he'd done to me? Two wrongs didn't make a right, but it damn sure felt right when I was doing it. Things between us were starting to feel forced, and it shouldn't have been that way when you loved someone. But wouldn't the love come back once the hurt subsided? I found myself asking myself questions that I already had the answers to.

How long did I expect to keep waiting for the hurt to leave? Shit, it had been almost two years, and I was still mad about his infidelity even though I'd gotten my lick back. I had his back during the roughest times of his life. When he lost his father, he pushed me, and everybody else, away, but I still stayed and comforted him through his hurt. I still pushed back, showing him all the love and affection, he needed when all he did was push me away. Yet, that still wasn't enough to keep the nigga out of another woman's bed. That bullshit line he gave me about hurt people hurt people went in one ear and out the other. By the time he could process half of the stuff he told me that night, I had my shit packed and at the nearest hotel I could find.

You can do everything possible to make sure your man stays loyal to you but at the end of the day, only a man has control over his own actions. I didn't want to hear that bullshit lie that all men cheat because a man who's afraid to lose me will always stand ten toes down.

Here I was, ready to walk down the aisle with a man who really didn't know anything about the real me. His downfall was that he believed every fucking thing I told him and never checked. He was sitting here, thinking that I didn't have any family or siblings to invite to the wedding because I was put into foster care, but that was the furthest thing from the truth. I knew who my siblings were, even though my sister didn't know who I was.

So many times, I wanted to hop on a flight and go to the address that was given to me, but I always held back. Once the shit happened with me and Champ, I had my own life to worry about. Looking for a sister who probably wouldn't believe shit I said wasn't at the top of my list. After that, so much time had passed, it really didn't matter to me anymore. I wasn't a little girl looking for her family anymore.

"Earth to fucking Kira!" Mike screamed out in front of me. I really had zoned out and hadn't heard a word he said, but I knew he was probably still on the Champ topic.

"Mike, I really don't have time for this shit today. I have to get fitted for my dress and hit the nail shop before my big day tomorrow. Let me ask you one question. Why did Champ owe you that money?" I asked him the million-dollar question that had been on my mind since I got the money for him.

"Go handle your business, Kir," he spoke, deading the rest of our conversation before crossing his legs and turning on the TV.

He hated Champ, and it was time to dig deeper and find out why. I had already gone and taken ten thousand dollars from him for Mike, and that was risky. If he ever found out what I did, I knew our relationship would truly be over. A man could probably deal with cheating but taking his money to take care of another man was another story. Mike said Champ owed him that, but if he owed it to him, why couldn't he get it from him?

I didn't know what I had gotten myself into, but this shit was getting stickier and stickier. All of this was going to clash, and I was going to be the person sitting in the middle, not knowing shit. Champ had seen pictures of Mike before, but he never mentioned anything about knowing him. What the fuck was Champ into? I knew what Mike did; it was no surprise to me. I had been with Champ for years and not one time had him owing anybody come up.

I got up to hop in the shower. I wasn't about to get in my head today. I grabbed a towel and headed to the shower, leaving Mike on the sofa by himself. It was fine when he had questions but when I had questions, he went mute. I would soon find out the truth from one of the two — even if I had to tell on myself to do so.

Later that day

I was thankful that we had a nail shop and spa in the hotel. I was worn out from getting the things I needed for the wedding, and this wasn't even a big wedding. It was only going to be me, him, and Sean. You would think the way I was going about the day, it was a big family gathering. I wanted that but maybe in another lifetime.

My friends were just that — friends — but inviting them here would've revealed a truth I wasn't ready to let out about myself. Like I said, Champ knew me, but he didn't know me like he should know a woman he was about to marry. I guess you could call it the money or the life I was used to, but I wasn't about to go back to that life for nobody.

It was quiet and only one woman was in here with me. She was a pretty woman, and I was never the type of woman to discredit the next woman.

"How may we help you?" one of the women who worked in the shop questioned me, walking from the back.

"Yes, can I have a mani and pedi set?" I asked her, hoping they didn't make me have an appointment before they serviced me.

"Yes, she can get you right after her. Just take a seat." She motioned for me to sit in the seat behind the woman was was getting her nails finished.

I peeked over the woman's shoulder. I was a nosey person. I was just trying to check out the nail tech's work. I didn't like all nail techs' work but who was I kidding? Liking her work or not, I had no other choice at the moment.

She must've sensed me looking in her direction because she turned a little, looking both ways to see if what she was feeling was true.

"I'm sorry, I didn't mean to be all over your back. I was just trying to see her work. I'm not from here," I told her honestly.

"No, it's not a problem. I do the same. I just needed to get out for a minute, so I decided to come here and get some relaxation. The spa is next for me," she spoke, telling her business like we knew each other.

"Definitely understand the need to get some relaxation. That's exactly why I'm here, on top of getting married tomorrow."

"Ohhh, that sounds nice. Congratulations on the wedding," she spoke genuinely, and I continued to talk. I felt comfortable talking to this stranger, and I didn't know why.

"Thank you. I don't know if I'm quite ready to walk down the aisle, but it's too late to be thinking like that, huh?" I told her honestly as I shrugged my shoulders. I felt defeated now, like there was no other choice but for me to get married, and he didn't deserve that. Shit, I didn't deserve that either. I loved Champ. I was just no longer in love with him.

"If you're not ready, why are you walking down the aisle? If you don't mind me asking," she spoke, but I could tell she was trying to make sure she didn't offend me.

"Trust me, I opened this conversation. So, no, I don't mind you asking. I guess because I'm comfortable with him. I don't have to learn from anyone else. Go through troubles trying to learn a new man. I know him inside and out, and at a point in time, I loved him."

Shaking her head up and down, I could see she kind of understood where I was coming from, even if she truly didn't respect the way I was going about it. I didn't know her from a can of paint, but I liked her.

"I've told you my whole life story in seconds and haven't even told you my name. I'm Kira."

"I'm Nadia," she told me, giggling to herself. "You and me both. I can tell you're not the judgmental type. I'm sure I can give you a good laugh about my story."

I heard what she'd said, but I couldn't get her name out of my mind. It was so crazy because I knew of a Nadia, but I didn't think this was the Nadia I knew *No, it couldn't be*, I said to myself.

"Girl, anything that can get my mind off of my own situation is a win for me, but I doubt it's that bad."

"I came here from Mississippi to enjoy my birthday. Usually, I don't enjoy it because it's the same day I lost my parents to a car wreck. I met a guy in the elevator and ended up having a one-night stand and this morning when I woke up, I saw he left money on the dresser like I was a damn prostitute. I've never done this before you ask."

I was thinking that she didn't look like the type to do that but looks were deceiving. The beginning of her story was terrible to hear, but it also helped me realize she was somebody else because the mother of the Nadia I knew was alive and kicking.

"You came to Las Vegas, got fucked up, and made a memory. Don't stay too long on it and the money situation. Maybe he was just showing his appreciation through his pockets. That doesn't necessarily mean that he thought you were a prostitute. The way you're not complaining about the amount lets me know he wasn't cheap. I spoke to her honestly because nowadays, a nigga wasn't leaving a bitch shit but a nut after they were finished. If I was her, I would be thankful the nigga didn't dip on me and leave me empty handed.

She was thinking about it as she looked down to see her nails since they were finished.

"Hey, I know we just met, but I would love it if you could come to the wedding tomorrow," I asked her the question I had been wanting to ask her since we got comfortable in our conversation.

"Sure! Do you mind if I bring my best friend with me?"

"No problem at all. Can I ask you one last question, Nadia?"

She turned around before she headed out the door. "Where are you from? I know you said Mississippi, but if you don't mind me asking, what part of Mississippi?"

"Vicksburg. Why?"

Staring blankly, the pieces were starting to fit, but a lot of the pieces didn't match up to what I had. I got her number to let her know where to meet us tomorrow. Even after that, I would keep a hold of it. If push came to shove, she might've been the help I needed. I could tell it was time to truly find my sister because I would think she was everybody I ran across until I found her myself.

Chapter 13

Champ

I'd been awake, looking at the ceiling for a good hour after Sean closed my door. I guess whatever he wanted to talk to me about could wait because he probably just wanted to let me know he was about to head out.

I had bigger problems, though. I couldn't get her, or last night, out of my mind. The connection we had during sex was like our souls were tied. I said that shit sounded like a bitch, but there wasn't shit else I could compare it to besides that. I needed to get right and get right fucking fast.

There was nothing there for me, even if I wanted it to be. Even if it was another time and another place, Kira had been in my picture for the past four years now. My soul would be tied tomorrow to the woman I'd taken through hell. I damn near wanted to turn on that Jacquees and Dej Loaf song, "You Belong to Somebody Else" because I felt that shit in my chest right now.

I needed to get up and get out of this damn room quickly because as long as I was in this room, my mind would stay on her. I knew I was off my square. I hadn't even called Kira to check on her and make sure she'd made it in. I looked down at my phone to see if she'd called me, and I had no missed calls.

I tapped her name on my screen to call her. I heard the phone ring multiple times before getting her voicemail. I wanted her to answer so I could hear her voice. Maybe that was all I needed to get this girl from last night out of my damn head.

I tapped my phone again, hoping she would just pick up her fucking phone. She saw a nigga calling her ass multiple times. What if this call was a fucking emergency?

"Hello?" she answered lowly.

"Kira, why are you whispering?" I asked her. It sounded like she was in a damn hole.

"I'm in the nail shop. It's rude to be loud, Champ," she spoke back in a more even tone.

"I was just calling to make sure you made it to Vegas," I told her, trying to steer away from an unneeded argument.

"Fine time to call me, Champ. Why would I not be here? We're getting married tomorrow," she asked me with an attitude.

I didn't know what the fuck her problem was. All a nigga had done was ask her had she made it. Was her women intuition kicking in? Did she already know what a nigga had done? I needed to chill the fuck out; I was bugging out for no damn reason. I was gone fuck around and get myself caught up.

"You right, baby. I was just asking. You got everything ready to become Mrs. Hoodman?" I questioned her. I didn't know whether I wanted her to be or not, if I was being honest with myself.

"Um, not quite yet, but I'm going to get everything together before the end of today. How about you and Sean? Do y'all have everything ready?"

"Yes, we should be done by the end of the day. He stepped out for a second, but I'm about to go and get fitted now. Are you sure you don't have anybody you want to invite to the wedding?" I questioned her because I didn't want her to have just anybody there. I wanted her to have people who she cared about and who actually cared about her. She actually had friends in Atlanta. I didn't know why she didn't choose to invite them here with her.

Let her tell it, at first, they were coming down here for a bachelorette party. Come yesterday, she swore everybody had something to do or didn't get approved for their days off. I smelled bullshit, but I let her have it. That was why I wasn't telling her about me and Sean heading to the strip club later. I would never hear the end of that shit if I did.

She would bring back up my old ways and my old days, and I just didn't want to hear it. I knew how to control myself if need be. I wasn't too good at it from the looks of it, but it was just something about Nadia. I had turned down many women over this past year not to fuck up the newfound man I was becoming for Kira. So why did I fuck up now? I found myself having more questions than answers.

She said she had no family, but there was no way she didn't have anyone she could invite from her past to enjoy her special day with her. I knew all about Kira being adopted. She never spoke much on it, but nobody from way back then to now was suspicious to me. I stayed out of it and minded my business because family could be hell sometimes, and I didn't know their story.

"I actually met someone today that I invited to the wedding. I liked her and she had a good vibe about her," she told me shockingly. I'd honestly never saw Kira click with a person that fast, so I wanted to meet this person she spoke so highly of.

"Really? I can't wait to see who this woman is. There has to be something special about her for you to want her to witness this day."

"Yes, that's what I said. I'm going to let you get back to what you were doing," she told me, rushing our conversation.

"Love you, Kira," I told her, trying to convince myself more than her.

"Love you too, Champ," she spoke back, but it wasn't the same happy, cheery, *I love you* we were used to.

I hung up the phone with Kira with thoughts of this other woman still swarming in my thoughts. I grabbed some casual things out of the bags we had delivered and went towards the shower. I needed to get up and handle business. I would just shoot Sean a text, letting him know where to meet me.

I made it to Friar Tux. They had a variety of everything, even tuxes for kids. I didn't need anything special. All I came in here for was to get fitted for a cream tux and maybe throw in a little bow tie for an extra kick. Kira wanted us to wear some casual, brown dress shoes, which I had no problem with, but I knew Sean was about to have a fit with this shit. I had him in an all-white tux with cream inside and a cream tie with his dress shoes.

I had already called ahead of time to have our things ready, so the only thing we would have to do was make sure our measurements were correct and the tuxes fitted us well.

I waited behind the guy in front of me as he spoke with the gentlemen who I assumed was supervising the register at the time.

"She must be a lucky girl for you to run in here the day before for a tux," the guy asked him as he took his measurements of his shoulder.

"Yes, she means a lot to me. I'm willing to do whatever it takes to see her happy tomorrow," the guy responded.

I guess tomorrow is going to be a good day for me and him, I thought to myself as I continued to wait and listen.

"If it wasn't for her and her letters getting me through my jail time, I don't know where I'd be. There's something about knowing someone is on the outside waiting for you to get home and welcoming you with open arms. That makes you never want to leave their side," he spoke.

You could tell he had genuine love for whoever he was talking about, and I could respect that. I felt the same when my woman held me down through all of my trauma, pain, and hurt. She deserved the world. Now I was feeling like I was put in the right place at the right time. He was speaking on something I needed to understand again.

"That's a real man," I spoke up. I knew that wasn't my conversation, but I just had to let him know that I felt completely where he was coming from.

He looked over his shoulder to acknowledge what I said with a head nod. Having bar, I'd seen a lot of people, but the guy in front of me looked familiar. He didn't say anything else once he nodded his head. We couldn't know each other.

I shot Sean a text, telling him to get his ass from wherever the fuck he was and come on. I knew the nigga didn't want me to marry Kira, but he knew what the fuck we had to do today. I didn't care if his tux was hanging off his ass like Soulja Boy; he was going to put that shit on.

The guy was finally finished, and it was time for me to step up and get fitted. I guess he would be getting his things later. "Whoever the lucky woman is, you make sure you cherish her forever. There's always somebody out there, looking to take what belongs to you," the guy spoke as he headed out the door.

I didn't know where that came from, but I didn't like the feeling his words gave me. His statement sent chills down my body because I couldn't picture Kira with anybody else. Yes, I may have stepped out, but I never wanted to lose her. That was my problem. I knew she would never leave, or so I thought.

"Hey, I called in an order to be sized for Champ Hoodman," I told the guy as he went to the back to get my things. My mood was fucked up now, and I just wanted to get the fuck up out of here.

Coming to the front with the plastic garment bags I went to try it on. I had to give it to him; I didn't know how long he'd been doing this, but my tux fit me like I was about to step into GQ magazine. Nothing needed to be altered, but I still stepped out to let him check everything out for me. This was my first time getting married, so I didn't want anything to go wrong tomorrow.

"Man, you really out did yourself with this altering," I complimented him as I stepped out of the dressing room. He nodded his head in approval as I stepped out, letting me know that I was good to go.

Sean still hadn't made it. I decided to just grab his tux and shoes with mine.

"Hey, you can ring all of this up for me. I can take it to go now," I told him as I walked back out of the dressing room with the clothes back on the hanger like I first received them.

I sat the things down on the counter, waiting for him to wrap them up so nothing could get on them before I headed back to the hotel.

"What's the total for me? "I asked him again, irritated.

"There's nothing left to pay. The guy before you paid for it. He said that it was a wedding gift from him," the guy told me.

I didn't like for a person to do that type of shit for me. Call it stubborn or whatever you wanted to call it, but I didn't like for a person to feel like I owed them anything, even though he didn't know me, and I didn't know him.

"Does he have to come back to pick up his items?" I asked him.

"Well, no. He has us sending his items to his hotel room," he spoke, stuttering a little like he didn't want to reveal the information.

"Pulling enough money out of my pocket, I instructed him to put those bills into the man's jacket pocket. I appreciated it, but I was good.

"Do you happen to know the guy's name?"

"Yes, he told me if you asked the name just to let you know that he would be seeing you again soon." He answered by placing the money under the counter. I figured he would probably keep it, but that wasn't my problem. I paid my dues back. Whether he received it or not was up to the guy.

He said I would be seeing him soon – whatever the fuck that meant. So when the time came, I would address the situation to him as a man. He probably meant well, but where I was from, nothing came easy like that, especially from a stranger.

I was actually glad Sean wasn't here because his temper was like a bubble, and he wouldn't have liked that at all. He would have felt the same way — like a nigga was playing in our faces. I could hold and take care of my own.

With all of that going on, I had forgotten to order me a damn Uber. I didn't see too many taxis down here at this part of the strip. I knew it was a no to call Kira for a ride because if she was at the nail shop, she would be there another hour or two before she was finished. She never got the bare minimum.

The weather was nice out here. I took off walking in the direction of the hotel. It was on the other end of the strip, which would only take me about thirty minutes to get to. I still hadn't gotten a chance to see what this city had to offer yet, but I would tonight.

The only thing I had done was sit in the hotel and do things I had no business doing and still, here it was again, her consuming my thoughts. What was it going to take for me to get her off of my mind? Maybe I just needed to stop by her room. All I wanted to do was to let her know the real about me and get her name.

Seeing a taxi waiting on the side of the street, I quickly walked to it, and my tour was over just that fast. I had to see her one last time before I said I do.

Chapter 14

Jayda

I walked out of the bathroom to find an empty ass room. I was beyond frustrated and pissed off that Nadia had actually left without saying a word. It wasn't like we were somewhere where we knew everybody or could easily find each other. Even if Nadia left out of the daycare without me knowing, or if I pulled up to her house, I would still know exactly where she was. It was just that easy.

How the hell would I find her here? When I didn't even know where I was my damn self. Ughhh! Nadia was really moving differently out here because normally, I would have to drag her out of the house to go anywhere. Here, she was leading the fucking way.

I didn't even know the reason for her running off like a thief in the night. All I knew was I told her to give me a second to hop in the shower and get dressed, and we could start our day. I knew I took a minute in the shower and got dressed, but it was just hitting noon. Here I was, taking a quicker shower than I normally would only to come out to nobody here. We had more than enough time to go and venture out around here. I really was bugged out that she couldn't just wait for me. Now I was even madder that I could've taken my normal hour prepping myself.

I reached over on the bed, still in my bath towel, to curse Nadia's ass. I picked up my phone and slid directly to her name in my phone. Frustrated as hell, I was pinching my lips together as my phone continued to ring, waiting on her to pick up. Hearing her phone go to voicemail irked me because I knew for a fact Nadia wouldn't go anywhere without her phone. That let me know that she was purposely ignoring my call. Throwing the phone down, I was going to wait till she gave me a call back. I wasn't about to kiss Nadia's ass, and I had no reason to.

Why was she ignoring my damn calls? I glanced around the room, looking as if the room could answer my questions for me. I knew she couldn't be this upset over me taking my time in the bathroom; she knew me too well for that.

I heard my phone ringing and rushed to grab it, thinking it was Nadia calling me back.

"Hello?" I answered quickly.

"Hello?" I asked again, finally looking at the phone to see that it was an unknown caller.

That was another problem I was having. I didn't understand why all of a sudden, this past month, I had been getting so many unknown calls. The same thing over and over again. No one would say a thing once I answered the phone.

"Why are you calling me?" I asked whoever was on the line. I hoped they would say something so I could see if it was a man or a woman calling.

"Jayda J," I heard the caller's soft voice saying, but there was no way it could be her.

I hung my phone up instantly after hearing her call me that. How could she have gotten this number? My mother was the only person who called me by that name, but I haven't heard from her since the day I was taken. There were times I wondered if she was okay, if she ever thought about me, or hell, if she was even alive. I left behind anything or anybody that could have answered those questions for me.

It seemed like my past was starting to catch up, just like I thought it would. The only thing I was wondering now was what secret would come out next. That phone call had put me in a feeling I couldn't even really describe. I didn't know if I wanted to be happy, sad, or mad with her. I really couldn't blame her for leaving me in that house. Being taken into foster care was better than waiting on my mother to bring me my next meal when she could or eating things I knew she had gotten out of the dumpster. When you were hungry with nothing to eat, trust me, you could eat anything, no matter how gross it was.

Maybe it was time to stop running from my past and face everything and everybody. The first person being my mother. I needed Nadia, and I needed her fast. I couldn't tell her everything, but I could tell her some things. Right now, I just needed my friend to vent to and her shoulder to lean on.

I went into the bathroom to throw on something quickly to head to the bar. I really didn't care about a light beat to my face. I threw on a two-piece casual bodycon jumpsuit, my Nike socks, with a pair of all black Nike Vapor Max. I was wearing my hair in its natural, curly state. I grabbed my purse to head down to the lobby. I was hoping to run into Mr. Kevin Hart Junior again. I could tell he was a good listener and not a judgmental person. He sat there and basically told a stranger that he was trying to catch his best friend's girlfriend cheating. You didn't get more honest than that.

I grabbed my room key and my black Michael Kors bag off the dresser before heading out the door. I pressed the button on the elevator for it to take me down to the lobby floor, where all the restaurants and the casino floor was. I didn't care how much sympathy I needed. I wasn't taking my ass over there to the janky ass slot machines again. I was sad; I wasn't stupid. I was keeping my coins in my pocket. They had gotten all they were going to get from me.

Hearing the elevator ding to stop, I looked at the numbers

that were beside the elevator door. I knew there was no way I was down to the lobby that fast. We were on one of the top floors. The doors opened, and I didn't know if I was being punked or what down here in Las Vegas, but these men had me wanting to line them up and choose like I was in a buffet line.

I tried not to stare as he entered the elevator. Taking my phone out of my purse, I clicked the Facebook app on my phone to keep me from looking up. I could see I had notifications that I hadn't checked yet. I clicked on Nadia's name since it said she had loved a comment of mine.

Before it could even load, I heard the elevator doors opening. I dropped my phone back into my bag and stepped out in front of the guy. I could tell he was a gentleman because even though the door had opened, he waited for me to get off first. He was a winner in my book because you didn't see men with manners too often.

I headed straight to the bar. I wanted a shot of Hennessy or Patrón quick. I knew by the end of the night, I was going to be in trouble. I didn't want to leave this bar until all of my problems had been washed away, I was back living the life where nobody knew anything, and my past stayed buried.

It was an hour later and here I was, with no call back from Nadia after calling her again another three or four times. I stirred my straw into my amaretto sour. I was on my umpteenth drink, and I knew sooner or later, the waiter would tell me I had reached my limit. I wouldn't even be mad or make a scene because I knew from the numbness of my face that I was at my limit.

"You know there're a lot of men in here that would take advantage of you and your situation?" the guy told me, sliding in the bar stool next to me. "Can we get her a glass of water?" he instructed the waiter.

"And you're not one of those guys, huh?" I questioned him, really not wanting to be bothered. Any other time, I would have flirted back, but I just wasn't on that type of time right now.

"Nah, I'm not pressed for a female or about a female. You don't have anything I want to take that I can't get for free. I've done my time, and I don't plan on going back anytime soon.

"What you're telling me is, I'm sitting here talking to a killer?" I asked him boldly.

"Woah, who said I was in jail for killing anyone? You see the tattoos all over my body, and you scream killer. I should be offended," he answered nonchalantly.

"Well then, was it drugs?"

"Damn, are you the police?" he spoke back with a slight grin on his face.

I was glad to see that he grinned a little because I thought he was offended by all of my questions and even though I wasn't looking for anything from him, I did like his company.

"Sorry. I'm glad I didn't offend you. I can be a little nosey at times."

"A little?" he asked, raising his eyebrows. "Since you asked your questions, my turn. Why are you over here drinking like your life is over? I've kept my eye on you and not in a weird way," he asked me bluntly.

I felt safe in his presence, so I answered him honestly. Today, I got a call from my mom. I haven't talked to her since I was taken into foster care, and I have no idea how she's found me.

"Is her finding you a good thing or bad thing? If it's going to interrupt your peace, no matter who it is, leave the problems where they are," he spoke honestly, and I really appreciated it.

I thought he would be like, 'she's your mother; you should forgive her.' That was something I didn't want to hear because even though she was my mother biologically, she didn't make me the woman I was today.

"That's the thing. I don't know if she's still the same person from before, or if she's a changed person. The old her, I want nothing to do with. If it's an addiction-free her, I honestly still don't know," I spoke freely.

"You won't know until you try. If she's not what you expected her to be, then get up and go on about your life but if she is, forgive but never forget," he told me as he got up from the chair to leave.

"I enjoyed your company. Can I at least get your name before you leave?" I asked, not trying to sound desperate. He was really a cool guy.

"You should pay more attention. I'm stored in your phone as Mike," he told me as he headed out of the bar. Now his ass had me wondering if he was a thief or something because how the hell did he put his number in my phone without me seeing and I'm sitting right here in front of him?

I was praying he wasn't a damn klepto because I liked his vibe. I could do the drugs if that's what he went to jail for, but I couldn't do a damn robber. I had to check my purse to make sure it was just my phone he went into. By his looks, he didn't look like he was pressed for my little coins, but you never knew. I laughed to myself. See, that was my problem. I didn't take anything seriously.

I headed back up to my room to take a quick nap. I was still a little tipsy, and a lot was on my mind. Hopefully, Nadia would stop by on her way to her room.

Chapter 15

Sean

I walked back and forth in the room. I was really bugging out, not in a bad way, though. More curious to know how this shit could happen. It was just crazy how after all this time, the nigga fell right out the air in Vegas with Kira. These were supposed to be the happiest days of my nigga's life. I was still trying to stall on telling Champ this shit until I had some more information about the situation. At the same time, I didn't want to leave him out here blindsided either.

I hated when a person felt like they had a fucking one up on me and right now, he did. I didn't know what he had planned, how he knew that I was the one who got his shit a few years back, or if he even knew. All I knew was that I had to be prepared for the worst. Mike wasn't a man you could push over but shit, neither was I. Pussy didn't pump through my blood just like it didn't pump through his. With both of our pop off mentalities, this shit was bound to end badly, and I didn't want Champ anywhere near this.

Last time I checked, he had almost five years to spend in prison. That was the reason I hit the lick in the first place. I knew it would be a minute before he got back out or even found out who had touched his shit. It wasn't hard to find out that I took over the streets once he left them.

What I got from him was only half of what put me on. I can admit as a man, I wouldn't be where I was if I didn't rob his trap house.

Thinking back

"Have y'all heard about Mike getting picked up with some dope and guns in the car with him?" Some dude rushed up to our dice game, informing us.

"Nawl, Mike don't move like that. I know that's some set up shit," I heard another dude saying from the crowd.

"They say he had enough on him to get him booked for life," the same guy who brought us the information said.

Here I was, sitting off to the side, making up my own master plan. A lot of these niggas didn't know anything about Mike but was speaking on the situation. I knew all too well how the streets went, so in order to know something, you had to damn near go to the source to get the information, wait for it to hit the paper the next day, or the news by five if it wasn't too late.

Everything you heard wasn't always true. I had been watching Mike and following him for the past two weeks — not to rob him. I wanted to see how he moved to be as big as he was. Men feared him, hoes wanted to be next to him, and the fiends craved what he put out on the street. All I wanted was a way to approach him to get on his team. I thought about starting my own shit, but I knew there was no way to be bigger than the man in front of me. I would always be the second competition, and I wanted it all. Nobody remembered number two, and I knew the fiends would only come to me if they couldn't afford what he was offering.

I headed away from the crowd to head home to see if anything was on the news yet. They loved to report shit in Vicksburg and be on the scene in seconds for catching a drug dealer. It was like catching them was more of a priority than murder. You would get more time selling dope than killing people here. Shit was truly sad.

It was five-thirty p.m., so I knew in about thirty minutes, it should make the six o'clock news on their breaking story. Wasn't shit else going on around here to top that.

I had enough time to put up the money I'd won at the dice game and hop in the shower. The little one-bedroom room I stayed in was cozy. It wasn't the best, but it got the job done.

By the time I got out of the bathroom, I made it right on time to catch the breaking news pop up at the top of the screen.

Mike's picture popped up on the screen. In bold letters, it read, 'One of the biggest dope men in Vicksburg, Mississippi picked up today with 500 grams of methamphetamine with a street value of $50,000. And, a semi-automatic gun was found in his possession.'

Damn! There was no way he'd got caught slipping with all of that shit on him like that. That shit smelled like a set up, but it wasn't my business. It was time for me to do what I needed to. It was time for the streets to know exactly who the fuck Sean was.

I picked up my phone because there was only one person I trusted with my life to do this shit with me. He wasn't into this street shit, but I knew he would do it because I asked him to.

"What up?" Champ answered on the first ring. I knew he was still taking losing his father hard, so I was hoping he looked out and said yes.

"Man, I need you to come run through and handle this shit with me. I'm telling you now, there's some risk in this shit if we get caught, but I don't think we will. I've been watching this nigga for a while, and it's like he don't trust anybody. He picks up his product from one of his dope houses alone and distributes it to each house. We just have to get to that house before he makes his first phone call," I told him, giving him the rundown on everything quickly because we didn't have a lot of time to waste.

"Fuck it. Scoop me from the house." I knew that was only his 'I don't give a fuck' demeanor talking, but I'd roll with it and make sure nothing happened to him. I would never be able to live with that shit.

I picked Champ up and gave him the rundown on what we were going to do again. I wanted to make sure he had the plan down pat and if anything was to happen, he was to leave me. I knew he wouldn't, but I would give my life for my nigga if I had to because this shit was on me.

We sat at the corner in a beat-up Honda I had hot-wired from a neighborhood. I had already taken the license plate off the car. I just wanted to wait till nightfall to get in and out. There was too much movement on the street in the daytime, and I didn't know who the fuck he had watching his shit.

"Nigga, can we get this shit over with?" Champ asked, bitching from the side for the third time. This nigga had no fucking patience at all. He acted like we were just walking up like, "Hey, how are you? Is anybody in this dope house?" His ass was really bugging, making me regret even bringing him.

"Nigga, come the fuck on. You already fucking up the plan. Time had gone back, so it was already dark at six. We crept down the block because we were parked up five houses down. We went through each backyard and with every backyard, I prayed they didn't have a fucking dog.

"Nigga, didn't you play some type of sport? Come the fuck on," I told Champ's ass as he was lagging behind me.

We were finally about to go to the yard that we needed. We peeked over the fence to make sure he had no traps or cameras surrounding the house. The camera wasn't a problem with the ski masks we wore. Looking around, I knew this shit couldn't be this easy, or I would've come alone. Either he was the dumbest nigga I knew which I doubted, or he just really felt like nobody around would touch his shit.

When I felt like the area was secured and no cars were coming, we quickly hopped the fence. Rushing to the back door, I twisted a knob just to see if it would open.

"FUCK THIS SHIT!" Champ said before kicking the door in. I was for sure gone get in this nigga's shit because I didn't need this loud shit.

I needed time to look and check the house to see where or if anything was here.

Now he had gave me a time frame I needed to be in and out with the noise he had just made. If fire could come from my head right now, I knew it would. Brushing past him, I bumped his shoulders purposely.

"Since you want to be Incredible Hulk, check the fucking closet, or if you feel any loose boards on the floor, raise them quickly, nigga!" I yelled at his ass. It was no use being quiet now; shit, if anybody was listening, they for sure would have heard the damn door. If that was the case, we had probably minutes before people came, guns fucking blazing. I knew Mike wasn't somebody to fuck with, but Champ didn't.

I moved the TV stand as it wiggled and knocked it to the ground. Fuck it. Seeing a board under it, I moved it to see three duffle bags.

"Bingo," I said to myself.

"Champ, come the fuck on, nigga." I grabbed the two bags as he grabbed the last one. I had no time to look. We hauled ass out of that front door without looking back. Throwing the bags in the car, I hopped in and sped off. All you could hear were the tires screeching.

My heart was beating a mile a minute as I kept checking behind me to see if anyone was following. I dropped the car off two blocks from where I had my car parked and headed home. I couldn't wait to see what the fuck were in those bags. All I could feel was that a nigga was about to get paid.

Grabbing the bags from the house, I looked around before heading in, adjusting the Glock 45 on my hip, just in case somebody wanted to try something. I could tell I was still on the edge. I never looked around like a crackhead watching for the police in my life.

I unlocked the door to the apartment, quickly going straight into the bags. I felt like a kid on Christmas, opening presents as I saw the bricks neatly wrapped. Opening the next bag, it was also full of bricks of cocaine. Looking over to Champ to see what was in his, he pulled out bands of money wrapped up. I knew this was the beginning of a takeover.

"You know I'm not a pussy, but I'm not into this drug shit. I always saw myself with a little bar and shit," he told me, speaking what I already knew.

"Say less, my nigga. I really appreciate you even sticking your neck out for me. That bag is yours to make whatever you want to do come true and to put your mom in something nice." I knew it was a shit load of money in that bag, but I knew what the fuck I could do with these bricks in front of me. I knew once the same product started to come out, people would have questions, but I would deal with that when it came.

Now I was sitting here, trying to figure out a way to tell Champ that the *I don't give a fuck* mind set he had back then was long gone. He was more levelheaded. He didn't have anything to worry about because my word was my bond, and I meant exactly what I said back then. I would give my life for him at any given moment, but there's no telling what I would do to that bitch Kira. It was always supposed to be death before dishonor, but I knew even if he found out what she did, he wouldn't want her dead. I, on the other hand, would go home and sleep like a baby. I didn't give a fuck about her.

I had to go somewhere to get my mind right because sitting here, thinking about a situation that I couldn't change was going to send me to my grave earlier than expected. I thought back on the girl from the other night, and she was just what I needed. She wanted me in the worst way and tonight, her wish was going to come true. There wasn't shit better than fucking to get this frustration out of me.

I threw on some grey Nike jogger pants, a white t-shirt, and slid on my Nike slides. I didn't need to dress up just to go a few floors up. It was about two p.m., so I was hoping she hadn't left out yet. I just needed about thirty minutes to bust this nut, and she could go about her way. She could have more of me if she wanted, but that first nut was coming quick.

The suite had two bedrooms in it. I stuck my head in there, trying to see if Champ was awake before I headed out. I wasn't just being overly cautious checking up on a grown ass man in his room; I needed to talk with him about some other shit too. The girl he'd met down here had him in his feelings, and he didn't even have to tell me. I listened to some of the things he'd been telling me, even when he thought I didn't. I just didn't want to voice my opinion too much because he knew I didn't like Kira and by that alone, anybody else he pursued would get my vote. I closed the door and headed out the front door.

I made it up to her room within ten minutes. I was hot and ready like Little Caesars, and that shit was bad business for a grown ass man like myself. I needed to be in something warm. I knocked on the door, not even thinking if she had somebody else in the room with her. I knocked again, thinking maybe she didn't hear me. After sitting there for a minute, I decided to take my ass to my room and try a hot shower.

As I was headed to the elevator, I heard her call out to me.

"Sean," she called out in a whispering tone. If we weren't the only ones out here, I wouldn't have heard a thing she said.

"Hey, I know it's kind of out of the blue, but do you got some time for a nigga like me? I promise to make up for last night," I spoke flat out what I wanted to do so there was no confusion. Yes, I would lay up and cuddle with her after, if that's what she wanted.

Not even saying a word back, she pulled the door open wider, motioning for me to come in. That was all the fuck I needed. I headed back in that direction, speed walking, before she changed her mind.

She turned to walk away, leaving me to close the door. I kicked it with the back of my foot as I walked in behind her, catching up to her stride before she could even get to the bed, I wrapped my hand around her throat, giving it a slight squeeze, nibbling from her neck to her ear.

"Shit." Hearing the moan escape her mouth was all I needed.

I turned her body around so that we were face to face with each other. I wasn't a man who kissed everybody, but her big, pink lips were glistening for me to put my lips on them. I took my time as both of our tongues met each other, kissing her while removing her jeans with my other hand.

I pushed her down on the bed with a little force, not too much. Seeing her grin, I knew this was about to be a fucking lunch session she wouldn't forget. I pulled her thong down her legs, and she removed her top. She was as ready as I was, and that shit made my dick brick up.

I climbed on the bed with her, kissing from her stomach on up to take my time with each nipple. One by one, I placed her nipple in my mouth and pinched the other nipple to give it the same attention.

I let my hands begin to travel and find the place I was waiting to enter, sticking one finger in and out each time coming out drenched. Her pussy was leaking, and I knew she was ready for me. Placing my thick hard dick inside of her, I could hear her gasp a little.

"Fuck," I had to let out.

Her pussy was tight and gushy, like her shit hadn't been touched. I knew what I came for, and that slow grinding wasn't about to happen right now. I grabbed both of her legs, putting them in the crooks of my arms. Hitting her with deep stroke after deep stroke, I could see her eyes start to roll into the back of her head.

"Talk that shit you were talking about last night, Jayda," I commanded.

"I can't, shittttttt! Right there. Right there!" she screamed out like she was speaking in tongues.

I gripped her ass, squeezing it, giving me more access to give her all of this dick. I didn't know if we would fuck again or see each other again, so I wanted to make a fucking impression. I felt her starting to throw her ass back on me, and I was ready for the ride.

"Damn, Jayda!" Slapping her ass, I knew I was about to nut soon. The grin on her face had her thinking she was in control, and I was about to change the fucking game.

I stopped mid stroke. "Turn around, Jayda." I wanted her to throw that little ass she had for me back. She did as I told her. I looked down to see her with a perfect arch as she turned her head sideways on the pillow, trying to catch her breath. She lifted her ass in the air a little. I sat back to let her take control since this was what the fuck she wanted.

I slapped her ass as she constantly threw her shit back. "Fuck, Jayda. Who taught you that shit?" She threw her ass in a swirling motion. You would have thought Jayda had a dump truck of ass behind her. She had me mesmerized with the shit she was doing. Nobody could ever tell me after this that a woman with a small ass couldn't throw that shit back better than one with a big ass. Jayda could give them a fucking run for their money, and I think her ass was about to trap me.

"Shit, Seannnnn! I'm about to nut!" she screamed out.

I wanted to tie her ass up and take her back to the A with me. Feeling my nut on its rise, I pulled her head up to where I could tongue kiss her while I matched her pace. I gripped her hips to match the pace. All you could hear were both of our moans in the room as we came to our peak. Letting my nut skeet all inside of her, I looked down to see a little seeping out. *Fuck!* The condom had fucking broke. I wasn't about to ruin the mood, though. So, I continued to lay down.

I was in heaven. I really didn't give a fuck about shit right now, and that was exactly why I needed this. I laid down beside her, moving my arm open to welcome her to my chest. I guess she got exactly what I meant because she scooted over to me and laid her curly hair on my chest. I put my fingers through her hair as I drifted off to sleep. I would have to talk to Champ about this shit later.

Chapter 16

Nadia

Heading back to the room, I had to admit that I was feeling way better than I felt when I left Jayda's room earlier. My anger had gotten the best of me, and now that my nerves had gone down, I was feeling a little bad about how I left out of her room without saying anything. I had been ignoring all of her calls. She could have been calling me about something serious and here I was, dodging every call because I was upset with her.

What if something bad was happening and I ignored her call? I wouldn't know what to do if something was wrong with her for real. I left the nail salon and headed back upstairs, ready to hear her curse me out, but she needed to hear what I had to say also. I wasn't completely wrong, and I would admit to that part of it. I just really didn't want to go back to the conversation about Aliza.

It seemed like she could do no wrong in Jayda's eyes, and I was over trying to make a person see shit that was in front of them. Double tapping the elevator to go up, I stood there, waiting for the elevator doors to open. I stepped into the elevator quickly, hoping that I didn't see the guy from last night. I tapped the up button in the elevator quickly so the doors could close. I promise, I didn't want to see this man again. I still had mixed feelings about last night, and I just wanted to forget it. He did give me a birthday gift that I would appreciate for a while but besides that, I could do without.

I didn't know which situation was worse: him leaving the money on the nightstand or being so drunk, I didn't even get a chance to get his name. Or maybe he said it, and I didn't remember. Hell, I couldn't remember. All I know is, he would forever be *him* to me.

Seeing him stick his hand inside the elevator door to stop it made me wonder if he was crazy. What if his hand would have gotten caught inside the door while it was closing. He made it just in time to slip inside of the elevator before the doors closed. No words were said as he stared into my eyes. His breaths were unsteady before breaking our stare.

This was exactly why I didn't need him near me. I didn't think the way he made me feel in just a short amount of time was possible.

"I was calling out for you before you walked into the elevator," he told me, breaking the silence in the elevator.

"How could you call out to me when you don't know what name to call me?" I told him back boldly with as much attitude as possible.

He stepped off to the side to lean back on the wall. I guess you could tell he was starting to think about what I had said. Not one time did I hear anyone say Nadia, so I really wanted to know what name he could have been called me. I got mad instantly because I know the nigga didn't just give me a name.

"So, what name were you calling me by because I never gave you my name and you never gave me yours," I asked him again since it seemed like the cat had his tongue. I watched him closely as he slid his hands inside the pants of his jeans.

"You're right and you're wrong. No, I didn't call you a name. I called out, 'hey, hey, hey,' trying to get your attention. I thought you would have at least turned around to look around at a person yelling."

"No, I don't mind anyone's business who's not mine and still, you didn't even have the decency to ask me my name. The fucking nerve. First, you leave money on the drawer, pure disrespect, now this," I voiced to him, annoyed.

I knew I was over the conversation until he stepped out onto my floor and walked with me. I wasn't a stalker by a long shot, but I did know that his room wasn't on the same floor as mine. Seeing him following behind me, I decided to stop and have a conversation with Jayda after I got rid of him.

"How may I help you?" I asked him as he stood behind me, waiting.

"Just give me ten minutes of your time and then I'm gone. I promise," he spoke genuinely.

I opened my room door and stood off to the side. I didn't need to give him a walk-through; he knew where everything was. I was just ready for him to say whatever he needed to say so that I could never see this man again. My mind was saying that, but my mouth was watering at the sight of him.

He sat back staring at me while he bit the corner of his jaw. Everything about him turned me on, and I didn't understand how I could be so turned on by a man when I still didn't know his name, and it seemed like he wasn't trying to be on a first name basis with me.

"I didn't mean any disrespect by leaving the money. I didn't think you were a prostitute or anything; that was just a little birthday gift to you from me. I didn't want to wake you, so I sat the money there and left."

I sat there, not saying a word. I had already said enough as is. The girl from the nail shop said he probably didn't mean any harm and here I was, jumping the gun, thinking the worst. I couldn't wait to fill her in on this tomorrow when I saw her for her wedding.

"You can't really blame me on the name part because neither of us were interested in each other's names because I'm pretty sure you don't know mine either. Let's start over. I'm Champ."

Getting off the bed, I walked to shake his hand that he held out to me as he leaned forward off of the dresser. He had to feel exactly as I felt because there was so much space in between us in the room.

"I'm Nadia. This feels awkward," I told him honestly because even though I didn't know his name, I felt like I knew him inside and out. I knew that was a strong feeling, but I couldn't help the way I felt.

Walking back over to the bed, the room drew quiet again. You could literally hear a pin drop. As we stood here, staring at each other, we had no words to say once again. Yes, we knew each other's names, but I still had a feeling that a big bomb was about to drop.

I could tell by the way he was fidgeting with his hands on the dresser that he had something he wanted to tell me.

"I'm a big girl. You can go ahead and say whatever it is you need to say, Champ," I spoke honestly, ready to get this shit over with and out of the way. I was a big girl who had made her own decision without asking this man a thing.

I told myself I would enjoy my birthday, and that's exactly what I did. There was no need to dwell on it. An even exchange. I guess this was what a one-night stand with good dick felt like, and I knew this was going to be my first and last time having one.

"I never meant to hurt you, honestly. There was just a connection to you that I couldn't let go of. As much as my mind told me that shit wasn't right, I still couldn't take away that magnetic pull I had for you." He spoke seeming genuine, but my trust was so fucked up; you never knew nowadays. I didn't trust a thing a man had to say.

"Look," I told him, holding up my hand to stop this whole little pity party. I had one more day in Vegas before my plane left to Vicksburg, and this was not how I wanted my night to go.

"I appreciate any honesty you're about to tell me, but we will never see each other again," I spoke, walking toward the door, feeling the hurt in my chest as I spoke. I opened the room door, waiting for him to get the hint that all of this was over. As much as I thought I could take it, I couldn't, and I just wanted to get him out of my room so I could breathe. Nothing could hurt if I didn't see him again. This little façade I was having would end soon.

He walked toward the door, staring at me as if there was so much more to say, but there wasn't. The simple fact was it was good while it lasted. He placed a kiss to my forehead and walked out the door. As fast as he came, he had gone.

I was hoping that Jayda would excuse my bitch ways and have drinks because right now, I needed my friend. I had yet to tell her about any of this. It's funny how when I really needed her, I was ready to look over Aliza but before, I just couldn't get over her and her petty antics. I would apologize over drinks. She knew how I could get about her, so I was hoping she would go easy on me.

Chapter 17

Champ

I still couldn't get this feeling out of my mind. It was crazy that I felt like I was cheating on her when I had a whole woman here. I wanted to get the shit off my chest that I was getting married tomorrow, but she was right; it really didn't matter. After tomorrow, I would be a married man and jump on my flight back to Atlanta, and she would be whichever way she was going.

I stood and stared at her hotel door for another five seconds wanting to knock on it, but I was going to grant her, her wish. I knew I didn't mean her no good, so it was best to let her enjoy the last of her vacation without me and my problems.

I stepped into the elevator, ready to head to my room to get a drink.

"Hey, hold the elevator!" I heard somebody yell, but if I didn't know anybody's voice, I knew that was Sean's ass.

I held my hand in the door, waiting for him to catch up. I'd been blowing his phone up with texts, letting him know to meet up, and he was exactly where I figured his ass to be — laid up. I stepped back, allowing him to enter while I kept a mug on my face.

When he was in some pussy, his whole train of thought left him. I knew he didn't know why I was mugging his ass, but he was about to find out. I hoped his tux was a little too big, so I could clown him even more.

"Nigga, this is not the floor our room is on, so what are

you doing on it?" I questioned him, already knowing the answer because that was just how much I knew him.

"Minding my business. But the question is, why is a man, who's getting married tomorrow, on this floor?"

"That's not the point; we can discuss that later. Why weren't you up to get your tux fitted this morning? You know what tomorrow is. I got your shit, so if you come in that muthafucka looking like a clown, that's on you," I told him, so he'd know I wasn't feeling him missing out on today.

That was supposed to be some brotherly shit we did together. You only got married for the first time once, and I wasn't no female, but a nigga was trying to make memories with this shit too, and he missed out on it.

"You know we haven't done shit since we came here. You been M.I.A on a nigga."

"Yes, there's some shit we need to talk about but not here. I can see the hotel security thinking they about to get some tea off a nigga," he spoke, looking up at the camera then back at me.

This had gone from a conversation about our tux to something serious, and I wasn't with it. I had just left one situation to come to this one. This was turning out to be a fucked-up night before my wedding.

We got off the elevator, and as we headed to the room, his ass had the nerve to be behind me, lagging, like a child who was about to get chastised.

"Mane, come your ass on and stop dragging your feet, nigga. Since this conversation is so damn secretive, you couldn't say it in the elevator," I told Sean, never looking back.

By the time he'd made it in the room, I was already at the bar with a shot of Hennessy going down my throat. The burning sensation I felt going down my throat was the best thing I was gone get to relieve this stress.

"Pour me up one of them before we start this conversation. I'ma need that drink too. As a matter of fact, pour yourself another one to," Sean told me, and I wasn't for the playing.

"Get your shit yourself and hurry up with this damn conversation. You on some real secret ass hoe shit, and I'm not feeling it."

I studied his face, trying to see if this was a way for him to take time from me talking about him missing out on the suits, or if this was about something serious. I wanted to know what it could be about that couldn't wait because he knew I didn't get into any of his other business, and he never spoke to me about it. It had to be about the girl's room he had just come out of because besides that, we hadn't talked about shit else up here.

"Fuck it. Let's get this shit over with. I been holding it in long enough," Sean said, throwing his hands up in the air as he paced around the room.

"Okay, so you know the lick we hit a while back that put the both of us on?" he told me as I shook my head up and down, letting him know I knew what he meant. But again, what the fuck did that have to do with right now? That happened so long ago; we were over that shit now. I didn't want to talk about it because it brought back a fucked-up time in my life.

"I had been watching the front door, waiting to see if I would see Kira walk in." He stopped to look at me to see what my facial expression was, but I was still trying to see how Kira and what we did had anything to do with one another. He realized I still had no questions, so he went on.

"I saw her walk in, laughing, with the guy we robbed," he told me, but it was like I didn't hear what the fuck he said.

"I thought the guy we robbed was serving major time," I

questioned him, still not getting to the Kira part yet because I honestly didn't know what to say about it.

"Yes, that's what I thought too — until I looked up his MDOC number and saw that he had an early release. The type of money he had, I could believe that his lawyer found a loophole somewhere for him. You didn't hear the part about your Kira?"

"YES! I heard the shit, nigga, I'm not fucking deaf!" I screamed out to him while going off into my own thoughts.

Why was he here in Vegas? Did he want his stuff back? I couldn't be mad at Sean because I decided to go on that lick with him; he didn't put a gun to my head and make me do anything. And what if Kira was just walking by him into the hotel by coincidence? I found myself asking myself questions I should've been asking Sean.

"You sure Kira wasn't just walking into the hotel, and he was beside her, walking in too? And it's been a few years. That probably wasn't the dude we robbed back then. I know he don't still look the same way from when you last saw him," I told Sean because maybe he was just bugging out.

"I know a friendly walk by when I see one, and that wasn't no friendly walk by. They came in together, and she was laughing all over the nigga. There was nothing unfamiliar about the conversation they were having. I know you don't want to hear it, but the bitch is looking real foul, nigga," he got out before I hopped over the couch to get in his space.

"I understand you're mad, but what the fuck we not gone do is call her out her fucking name. She innocent until proven fucking guilty. Take that shit however you want to," I spoke, nose to nose with my nigga, a man who'd had my back through whatever but at this moment, he'd turned into an enemy.

"You mean to tell me you gone sit up here and go toe-to-toe with me about some shit I saw with my own eyes? This not a bitch that you were fucking coming to tell you about your girl. This a nigga who's been with you through thick and thin. You always tell me what pussy will do to me, but it'll make you turn your friend into a fucking enemy, nigga. I will never allow anything to happen to you, so I just advise you to watch your back while you here," he told me before he stormed out of the room, slamming the door.

Falling back on the couch, I rubbed my hands down the front of my face. What the fuck else did he think I was going to do? I was about to marry this woman tomorrow. There was no way I was going to allow the word of anybody to tell me something about Kira without me seeing it for myself. Even Sean. He wasn't the best candidate either. He sat right there and told me that he was waiting for her to walk in. He was looking for shit to find on her, and I didn't understand why.

I had put her through a bunch of shit, not the other way around. She was better off having somebody watch me here than me having somebody watch her. I had proven myself to be disloyal time after time and not one time have I caught her with someone.

Whoever this guy was had to have been prying on Kira because there was no way I could see her knowing that we'd robbed the guy and not even coming to me about it. She was too nosey for her own good, and she couldn't hold anything in to save her life. She would've been ready to throw that in my face.

I knew I would have to ask her about this before the wedding tomorrow. There was no way I could marry her without looking in her face and getting my answer. I picked up the phone to dial her number, but I placed it back down. This wasn't something you asked a person over the phone. I had gone against the grain on Sean. I was just hoping that I did the right thing, and I knew Kira like I thought I did.

Chapter 18

Mike

I had been out of jail for the past month, letting it be known to only a few. I could count on one hand how many people had seen me, but it was only until I made my next move. Everybody would know that the man of the streets was back and in full effect but before I could do that, I had somebody I needed to see.

I knew I had to come home and move different; they lived by different rules. I had only been gone for three years, but the game had changed. The streets weren't the same anymore. These young niggas didn't live off loyalty or not killing women or kids. For the right amount, anybody could get it and I didn't want anyone near me who felt that shit was cool. There were standards and morals to this shit, but I guess that was dead too.

Half of the guys I hung with or gave a job to in their time of need switched up and joined the other team. I didn't know who I could trust right now. I couldn't be mad because when you had a family to feed, you didn't give a fuck where you got your product from, as long you got it.

I just knew it would be harder to do what I had planned. I was taught to be a man and say whatever was needed to be said. Say the shit I had to say to say face to face, just like a man. I didn't want to cut corners and have anyone say anything for me. I wanted to talk to the new boss on the streets. I knew we had a lot to get caught up on.

I was coming back for everything they thought they took

from me without me knowing. The same day I went in, the pigs tried everything to get me to turn on anybody bigger than me, which let me know they didn't know shit because nobody was hotter on the streets than me. Once a fiend got their hands on anything that came from my name, I was sure they would be a returning customer. Nobody had it as pure as me, and there was a reason for that.

Sitting in the cold ass interrogation room, I didn't open my mouth to answer shit. There was nothing left to be said. I had slipped up, thinking with the wrong head while I had product in the car, and it got me here. Pussy was for sure something that could make the smartest nigga dumb. I couldn't blame anybody but myself and the extra dark illegal tint I had on my Tahoe that screamed, 'police, fuck with me.'

They had been looking for a way to get me off their streets as they called them, but I knew in due time, I would be back. The amount of money I paid my lawyer, Sweet, wasn't for no reason. He was the best of the best. I was caught red handed, so I knew I would have to sit and do some time; I was just wondering how he would work his magic to get me lower than football numbers because that's sure as hell what I was looking at right now.

After finally realizing I didn't have shit to say, they finally gave me my phone call. Calling my lawyer instantly, I was a little pissed because if the streets knew I was in here, it was his fucking job to know that I was in here also. I didn't need my lawyer to clock my every move, but he should've had somebody in this bitch tell him when the fuck his clients were walking through the door. The big-name ones at that.

He was there within fifteen minutes. I really wasn't rushing him; the shit I needed to say couldn't be talked about on the jail phone. I needed my product and my money moved as quickly as possible. I didn't trust or take anybody with me to my drop spot, but you never knew who was lurking in the shadows. I knew a nigga wasn't dumb enough to touch my shit, though.

Watching Sweet walk through the door, he looked behind him to motion for the officer to give us some privacy.

"Mike, you've dug yourself in a hole. You were caught red handed with the shit on you. How am I supposed to flip this?" he asked me to rub his bald head.

"I don't know. That's what the fuck I pay you to figure out. I let him know, not giving a fuck.

"Look, I need to see your phone to make a quick call," I told him, knowing I was pushing it, but I didn't trust his ass either. He might've gone to the house to try to take my shit too.

"You need a lot today, I see. Make it quick while I watch the door," he told me, sliding a burner phone across the table. This was why I paid his ass. Because who sits with a burner phone in their briefcase?

Dialing the number quickly, I hit up my boy, Bishop, to let him know the address and whereabouts of what I needed him to get. I knew it would only take him about twenty minutes to get there from Indiana Avenue. I sat back, waiting to get the okay before I could go to my cell and kick my feet back. This wasn't the first time I was in this muthafucka, and it wouldn't be the last if I made a dumb ass mistake again.

I picked up the phone as Sweet stood up quickly again to watch the door.

"Say the word," I spoke to Bishop before he could even get a chance to say anything.

"It's not here, Mike," he spoke into the phone.

"Did you check under the boards on the third house on that street?" I asked his ass again, making sure he was at the right house, but I knew he was at the right house. He knew the house just like me.

"Yes, I think I'm too late. Your back door was already kicked in, and everything was ransacked when I walked through the door. I still wanted to check your spot to make sure it was there, but the shit gone, bro."

"I didn't even go into questioning because whoever had my shit would hit the streets with it soon and when they did, they would fuck up. You couldn't copy me. So, if I heard about any good dope hitting the street that was just as good as mine, I knew then I had found who the fuck robbed me.

I wasn't a dumb nigga to leave all of my money and dope in one place, but I for sure wasn't sending a muthafucka to where I laid my head. Nobody knew that location, so when I got out, I would still be good. I slid Sweet the phone before the police came in to put my cuffs on.

"We have court in the morning. You know I'm going to do my best. Get you some rest," he told me as he patted my shoulder and walked off with his Italian suit with his Ferragamo loafers on. You would think the way I spoke of him that he was a black guy, but he was as white and crooked as it came, and I loved that about him.

I knew I wouldn't be sleeping well tonight because I needed to know who the fuck could have known about that house. I was slipping bad. I had to have niggas out here following me without me knowing, but why the fuck didn't he make his move?

Here I was with a million questions but not one fucking answer, and I knew it could take me a while before I got them. That was what was pissing me off the most. How the fuck could I lose my freedom, product, and some of my money all in the same day?

I got up and ready for court. I might have been guilty, but that didn't mean I had to show up to court looking that way. My mother was there as always with my three-piece custom-tailored suit and my Christian Louboutin shoes. I knew she had questions but Sweet knew she was only to know the bare minimum when it came to anything illegal with me. I hated to see my mother's face when my time was called out, but I had to give it to him; five years wasn't shit. I would eat that up and be back out to the street, gunning for whoever took my shit.

Within two and a half years, Sweet had come back to me, saying he had something that could get me off. I knew there was something fishy with the situation because I was caught red handed, but I didn't give a fuck. For the right price and the right judge, I was out and back on the street, and I now had a name.

It was quite funny that exactly what I said would happen, happened. Within a month, a new cat named Sean had hit the streets with shit just as pure as mine. I had never heard of him before, but I just wasn't a nigga who believed in coincidences. So, I had Bishop send one of my testing junkies, Liz, to his spot. She could tell you if it was good dope or bad, but I knew for a fact she could tell me if it was my shit.

When I got the call that it was a go and Liz gave him the head nod he was looking for, I knew me and Sean were going to have to have a talk. I wasn't the type to send anybody to handle my business. I didn't give a fuck if it took five years, I wanted everything that was taken from me and more. I had to give it to him; he kept a closed mouth because there was no talk on the street about him taking my shit. It was like he just popped up on the block with soldiers one night and the rest followed.

He thought he'd done something, pushing it off a month like I would've moved past it, but I don't move past losses — especially big ones. I got home and put my ears and resources to the street. I wanted to know all about him all the way down to where he went to eat. Now I realized how easy it was to be followed when you had no idea that a person was after your head.

Crazy thing about it, he moved a lot like me — well calculated, didn't use people to do his drops for him, he even moved around solo. I didn't know whether I wanted to rock his shit or make him my second in command. He was doing well for himself. My only question was how he found my connect. It was really funny how Julio never reached out to me while I was behind bars. He said fuck me the minute my time was handed to me, and I would never forget that. As much money as I made his ass, you would've thought he would've at least sent me something on the inside. I didn't need shit but damn, it was the fucking thought.

I followed him around, but it didn't seem like he lived that life; he was always going to a bar I could see he owned and back home. I figured I would sit outside his home to see if it was some kind of act, but I never imagined I would see her coming out of his door.

I'd told my mother I didn't want anybody to write me or know the jail I was at. When I got home, I would feel all the love everybody had to give me. I didn't need to be sitting in there, hearing everybody's sad stories when I couldn't do anything to change them.

I followed Kira from her home to Boston Supreme. As she walked back out from getting her food, I was sitting on her hood, waiting for her to notice me. The minute she looked up, the tears started, and I couldn't help but to admire how much she had grown in these years.

"Whennn did you come home?" she asked me, slightly stuttering her words. I knew she was surprised to see me out so early.

"I just got home. When doesn't matter. How has life been treating you?" I questioned her to see how much she would reveal to me.

"It's good. I'm about to get married in Las Vegas in a few weeks," she told me, lowering her head, but I couldn't say a thing to her. She was grown.

"Does he treat you right?" I questioned.

"He's a man; what do you think?" she told me, shrugging her shoulders. "But he does love me, and I know we can get past whatever," she spoke confidently.

"Give me your phone so I can lock your number in, and you can do the same," I told her, taking her phone out of her hand and inserting my number. I hit the call button to save her number and stepped away from the car. I knew I would be seeing her again, and she was going to be my way in. I hated to use her to get what I needed; I just hoped she forgave me when my true intentions came out.

Chapter 19

Jayda

After laying here from being dickmatized, I still couldn't get that phone call from my mother out of my head. Your mother was supposed to be your best friend. The person you went through life with, telling everything to, and mine just wasn't that for me, and I couldn't let that go.

If it was so easy for her to find me or my number, why wait this long? Life had been good for me, and I just didn't want to lose that. I heard a knock at my door and damn near twisted my ankle the way I sprinted to the door to open it. I was hoping Sean had dropped back by unannounced. I needed somebody to talk to again, just to get a second opinion on my situation. I was a grown person and could think for myself but in this situation, I was like putty in the middle of someone's hands. I didn't know how I wanted to feel.

I opened the door, this time without looking through the peephole. That was a big mistake because I saw that it was Nadia walking through the door. I stood at the door with my arms still folded and the door still slightly cracked. I knew Nadia didn't think she was going to waltz her ass in here after she ignored me all day.

"How may I help you?" I asked Nadia with so much attitude. I wanted her to feel all of my anger. I didn't want my friend to think shit was sweet because it wasn't.

Yes, we were used to getting mad and ignoring each other

for a moment; that's what friends did, but this case was different. Fucked around and got taken, I was not about to hop off bridges and cars to find her ass. She was good as sold to the highest bidder because she didn't have to act like that.

"Please close the door and let me explain, Jayda," she whined as I slowly closed the door, being dramatic as I headed to the chair across from the bed to take a seat.

"You look really refreshed. Nice mani and pedi," I told her, rolling my eyes because her ass could have waited on me.

"I thought your other best friend was going to fly out here and you two go since you can't seem to see her shady ass ways," Nadia spoke with the same attitude.

I knew all of this was not about Aliza.

"Seems to me you're the only one bugging about a fucking Facebook post. You allow her to get under your skin then that's your own problem. I'm not about to sit up here and explain which one of y'all are my best friend because you should know that answer already."

"Well, I kind of thought about all of that and realized I did go overboard not answering your calls. Anything could have happened and when I thought about it, I headed over," she told me like I was just about to let that ride.

"Fine fucking time for you to come, Nadia. It's nine at night. If somebody would have gotten me, they would have sent my ass off to Paris by now. That shit is not cool, and I keep telling you that. We went from you about to tell me about your hoeish night to me walking out to an empty ass room, getting my calls ignored," I stressed to her.

"You don't know how fucked up my day has been. I blew up your phone over and over, trying to talk to you about my problems, and you worried about somebody that's in Vicksburg while we in Las Vegas. Usually, you're the one with common sense, but you bugging today," I expressed, letting her know this was far from over.

The room got quiet with neither her nor me saying a word. There wasn't really anything left to say. She knew she was wrong, and had acknowledged it so I would let her be great.

"I said I was wrong, and I apologize, Jayda, damn. I even brought your favorite," she whined, pulling out the Hypnotic and Hennessy bottles.

She knew I couldn't turn down a good drink, but I still wasn't going to let her get out of this that easily. I would continue to throw my little slick comments out there, but I would lose the attitude by the time I was through with my first drink. I knew it and she did too.

"I still haven't gotten the chance to tell you about last night," she informed me as she mixed both of our cups together with a mixture of the Hypnotic and the Hennessy, making my favorite Incredible Hulk drink.

"You would've had you not wanted to worry about other things that wasn't important. But come on and tell me what made you turn into a hoe overnight. Mrs. Nobody is Worth Me Sleeping With on the First Night," I told her, telling her the exact words she'd told me.

"Yes, I really didn't expect for it to go that way. Here we were, vibing at the blackjack table and one thing led to another. He realized I was drunk and offered to walk me to my room. All I knew was I wanted that man, and I wanted him at that moment."

I could tell my friend had messed up. She'd done the one thing she wasn't supposed to do. She messed up and fell for the one-night stand dick. I wasn't going to put her on blast yet. I knew she wasn't done with her story.

"That man catered to me like he knew my body in and out. Everything was good until I woke up to money on the nightstand. I wasn't feeling that at all. I would've rather he just left without saying a word," she mentioned with her nose turned upside down. My friend had her boujie moments, but I understood this.

"Bihh, how much did he leave you?" I asked her seriously, trying to keep a straight face while I continued to sit from my cup.

"I didn't even count it; I just threw it into my purse."

Looking back, she grabbed her bag and pulled the bills out of her purse. You could tell from the way it looked, she had to have had close to a thousand dollars rolled up.

"See," she spoke, showing me the money out of her purse.

"Friend, I don't give a fuck if that man was paying me for my most prized possession or not. And you had the nerve to come in here with this little ass bottle of Hennessy. Nawl, I deserve a night out. Since you want to make up, tonight's on you and this time, when I get out the bathroom, bitch, you better not be gone," I told her, rushing to the bathroom to freshen myself up. I didn't have time to hear her mouth, so a hoe bath would have to do.

"Matter of fact, take your ass to your room; you can do a little better with your outfit too. It's still your birthday, friend!" I screamed out the bathroom door, trying to buy me some more time.

"Yeah, yeah. You have an hour, Jayda. You're not slick," I heard her commenting back as the door to my room closed.

As much as I wanted to talk about my situation, I wanted to do that with someone who didn't know me. I knew soon I would have to tell Nadia the truth about certain things in my life but tonight, we would enjoy ourselves. When we got back home and back to our regular scheduled lives, then I would have that talk with her. I trusted her with my life, so it was time she learned me inside and out.

I was walking out the bathroom right on time when I heard Nadia knocking on the door. I opened it to see my girl did not come to fucking play our last night here. If I would've known that getting her some dick would bring her out of her shell like this, I would've sent a chocolate specimen her way.

The way her dress hugged her curves and the see-through part on the side showed off her bare skin, I knew she couldn't have picked this dress out. The black strap around the heels she had on matched her outfit perfectly. She even went the extra mile to throw on some red lipstick. She was giving, and I was here for it. I hoped my friend kept this same energy when we went back home.

I decided to wear my black leather pants, a leather crop top, and my all-black, knee-length Steve Madden shoes. I threw on a nice Michael Kors watch and my black crop jacket, and I was ready to head out of the door behind her. I was never the friend who'd change because my friend was more dressed up than me. It was her night, and she was supposed to outshine anybody walking, included me and I loved it. I planned on hyping my friend up all night.

I pulled up Google on my phone because it was my best friend when I went to places and didn't know where to go or what place would have the crowd. I typed in *clubs to go to in Las Vegas* and waited for something to pop up while we headed to the elevator.

I did what any person would do; I chose the club with the most likes and stars. If it wasn't lit, then we would just have to go to another club. Club hopping would be fun too. I didn't care, as long as I could drink, I was down. We headed to the parking garage to the rental car. We hadn't moved this car since we had come to Las Vegas, and that was not the plan.

The XS Nightclub was only about fifteen minutes away. No conversation was needed in the car; we just vibed to the music and headed to enjoy our night. I looked over at Nadia rapping with GloRilla and smiled. If you knew how she celebrated her birthday every year, then you would smile for her too.

I pulled up to the club and knew this was exactly where we were supposed to be. The cars were lining the streets, and this made me very satisfied of my shoe choice for tonight. Nadia was just going to have to click her ass in them heels from down the street. Even Valet was packed, which let me know it was about to be hard for us to get a seat in here.

I pulled back down the block where I'd seen a parking spot and prayed nobody got it. Pulling into the spot, I looked over at Nadia because I could already read her face.

"Go ahead with the attitude. Nobody told your ass to wear those heels," I told her, not even giving her a chance to say what she wanted to say.

"I'm going to give you that, but just know I'm mad as hell," she told me before getting out and slamming the door.

"Lead the way and quit slamming these people's shit because I'm not giving they ass any extra for damages. I still got a picture of your card in my phone the minute they try to," I told her seriously, following behind her, snickering to myself.

I couldn't lie. This was a little way from the club, but I was sure we would enjoy ourselves once we got in. It took us about twenty minutes to get up the block because Nadia stopped every few seconds to lean on people's cars to take a rest. I was hoping one of the alarms went off on her ass. You wouldn't be able to pick me up off this ground how tickled I was going to be.

"Friend, I'm telling you now before you go in here. You only get one one-night stand before you give me hoe vibes," I informed her, giving her the side eye as we walked up to the lines. I had done the same exact thing she did, but I would fill her in with that later too. It was my time to get my laughs out the way.

"You two come with me." The guy from the door motioned for us to head into the building. I didn't even question him. My girl had stood long enough and whatever got us this past, I was thankful for.

The guy shocked me when he walked us into the building to a section that was roped off.

"Order what you'd like. He said he'll be right back in a second," he spoke as he headed back out of the section.

I guess me and Nadia were both thinking the same thing as she turned to look at me. I shrugged my shoulders because I had no clue who he was or who he wanted. I wanted to enjoy my night, and if this meant whoever this was wouldn't make us spend a dime, I was with it.

Before we could sit down comfortably, me and Nadia were on our feet.

I tell all my niggas cut the check
Buss it down, turn your goofy down pound
Imma do splits on it, yes, split on it,
I'm a bad bitch, I'ma throw fits on it
I'm a bust it open! I'ma go stupid and be ditz on it

Before I could even fully sit up completely from twerking, I could feel a hard figure behind me. I knew it wasn't a female by the way his manhood sat on my butt. I turned around to see who this mystery man was that was so comfortable with coming into my space.

I came face to face with Mike. His Giorgio Armani cologne tickled my nostrils. I loved a nice smelling man. Not only did he smell good; his simple attire tonight was it for me. You would've thought we were both in each other's closet with the matching all black. He had on a Polo button down with the red house, some back jeans, and a pair of red Jordan 5s.

"I see you checking me out. Do you like what you see? I want to know that answer before you start to get your liquor in you," he whispered in my ear since my back was to him.

I could see Nadia checking me out from the side with questioning eyes, but she wasn't the type to put me on blast in front of Mike.

"They say a drunk tongue tells no lie, though," I responded, looking straight forward onto the dance floor, trying not to give him the satisfaction. This man looked good, and he knew he did.

"Can I have you tonight, Jada? Answer me and I will continue to let you have your girls' night with everything on me."

"And if I say no, will you take the section and everything else away?"

"I'm not that type of nigga, sweetheart. I know how to take my lick like a man. There're plenty of women in here I can have, but I want you," he said like that shit was nothing.

"Well, if any woman in here can have you, go get them," I told him, stepping out of his embrace, but that did nothing for him; he moved right back into mine.

"That's the thing. I'm pretty sure I'm not the only nigga in here who wants you, so don't take that comment to the head. Yes or no? I'm not the begging type, Jayda, but you got me ready to get on my knee in here in front of everybody, and I don't even know you.

"You talk a good game, but I can read through you. The number's in your phone, sweetheart. Use it." He spoke confidently as he walked off into the crowd.

Damn, I had the nerve to tell Nadia if she fucked two niggas, she was a whore, and here I was, about to do exactly what I told her not to do. I turned around to see Nadia sitting on the couch in the section, and I knew it was time for me to fill her in on this.

"Speak, hun. Y'all's body language was a little too familiar. You fucked him, huh?" she blurted out before I even sat down.

"Well, damn. Read me then, Mrs. Nadia. No, I did not fuck him yet," I told her honestly because he was definitely about to catch this good stuff before I left tomorrow. I wanted to think about this weekend for a long time. I went from not having sex in a year to fucking two niggas in a weekend. I was a bad girl, and I needed my ass whooped.

"Which means you're going to. I must admit, he is nice looking and ripped. What happens in Vegas stays in Vegas, sis," she told me, holding her cup up. I didn't even know they'd brought anything to the table, or I would have stopped talking and answered him a little sooner.

"Speaking of what happens in Vegas stays in Vegas, I see your guy from the elevator is approaching," I grinned to myself, ready to see how this interaction would go. If she would've seen her face, she looked like she had been caught cheating.

This night was getting juicy, and it was only the beginning. It looked like I wouldn't have to bail out on my friend after all. She would be in good hands. She gave him the pussy already, so I knew he didn't have to take it. It was almost midnight, but they partied all night in Las Vegas.

"Nice to meet you. I'm champ. I take it you're the friend to this stubborn woman beside you," he said, finally saying something after he realized that Nadia wasn't going to look up at him.

"Yes, that would be me, and stubborn would be an understatement. Let me scoot over this way so you can get a seat next to her," I told him, being the messy friend. I didn't have to look over to know Nadia was mugging me, but one more night of good dick wouldn't hurt her.

"After we've done all that we've done, I think a hi would be okay," he told her, making her more uncomfortable than he knew.

"Yes, and we said all we needed to say in the room. There's nothing left to talk about," her rude ass muttered back. He didn't know it, but he had to come hard to move her. Once she went into bitch mode, there was no changing that.

"Yes, but you would have also felt a way if you saw me in the club and I acted like I didn't see you," he told her.

"You definitely are reading her right now," I sat up, putting my two cents in before I continued listening on.

"No, I wouldn't have, Mr. Champ."

"If you miss a nigga, say that. I miss your pretty ass too," he told her for the win because he damn sure won me over with that line. I would've left right then and there.

"If you miss me, take me to my room," Nadia told him, shocking the hell out of me. The liquor had turned my girl bold. I could tell he didn't expect that either.

"As much as I'd love to, I have somewhere to be in the morning, and I'm truly sorry I can't," he expressed as he got up to leave.

I didn't know what to say to my friend. Hell, I didn't know what to say at all. How did their conversation go from sugar to shit in seconds? I knew he'd hurt my friend's feelings, but you wouldn't be able to read her face to know. She held in emotion easily.

"You ready to go, friend?" I asked her, not even trying to bring up the moment that had just happened because there was truly nothing left to say on it. He'd lost out, and he was going to regret it in the future. Nadia was the full package, and any man who couldn't see my girl's value was his loss.

He'd just fucked up the mood for everybody tonight because

now I wasn't feeling sending Mike a text. If it was meant for us to see each other again before I left Vegas, then it would happen. Tonight, I was going to be by my friend's side. I brought her here to enjoy herself, not let a man get her in her feelings.

"Yes, I'm ready. Speaking of places to go, we've been invited to a wedding tomorrow," she told me like it was nothing. How the hell were we invited to a wedding and we didn't even know anyone here?

"You went out today and made a friend while the main reason you were blocking my call was because you were in your feelings about me having another friend. If that's not the pot calling the kettle black," I told her, trying to lighten the mood a little.

"My fake friendship expires tomorrow. Your fake friendship will continue once we're home. We are not in the same boat," Nadia explained, rolling her eyes as we headed down the block to get the car.

I guess it would be nice seeing pure happiness tomorrow, even though I didn't know the woman. Las Vegas was where you see any and everything, and I was ready to see what tomorrow brought. The past two days had been eventful. It would be a surprise to me if tomorrow went how it was supposed to. We all had somewhere to be tomorrow. I just hoped Vegas was big enough to keep those two separated tomorrow because he had no chance anymore.

Chapter 20

Kira

My nerves were shot, laying in the bed this morning. I didn't know which emotion to feel. I didn't know what to do. I was just everywhere this morning. I knew I tossed and turned for hours. I was trying to make myself believe that wasn't a sign, but maybe it was.

I truly did have love for Champ. I just wasn't in love with him anymore. I even looked up on YouTube if you could fall back in love with your mate. Hell, everything was on YouTube. I was trying to get confirmation from anybody, even people I didn't know. I felt a little better because I wasn't the only person thinking of these questions. There were hundreds of videos, some agreeing that you could fall back in love with your spouse again and some saying that once the trust is gone, the love was something that really didn't matter.

I really felt the second one. How could you gain the trust of a person who had no reason to break your trust in the beginning? Someone you'd been there for time and time again, even when you didn't have to be. I just couldn't shake that hurt.

He had everything in front of him. Yet, he still fumbled the bag. I didn't believe that every man was a cheater; if a man truly loved you, he wouldn't do a thing to sacrifice your relationship. It would hurt him to see you hurt.

I'd heard him say I'm sorry a million times. His actions even showed that he'd changed, but it was a little too late. I was stuck between should I stay or should I go. I was really stuck between yes and no.

Hearing the water going in the kitchen made me get up. Mike was a big help. He listened to me, even though he didn't agree with what I was doing. He never stepped on my toes about it. Ever since he'd been released from jail, we'd been joined at the hip. I loved him more than he would ever know.

I got out the bed and slid my house shoes on. I had an hour before the lady came to the hotel to do my makeup and pin my hair up. Instead of having two people come to me, I decided to look up somebody here who could do both my hair and my makeup. That way, one didn't have to wait on the other or be in each other's way.

"Well, if it isn't the bride to be?" he expressed, being an asshole as he sat our plates down at the table.

"Don't start. I already couldn't sleep," I told him honestly.

"If you couldn't sleep, don't you think that's a sign He's trying to give you?"

"And what sign am I trying to tell you with this?" I cackled, throwing up my middle finger.

"Yeah, yeah, whatever you say," he exhaled, not even entertaining me this morning. I knew there was a lot more he wanted to say; he just didn't want to start with me this morning. He knew every one word he said, I'd have five more words coming back his way.

He was very overprotective of me, and I understood that, but I still felt like there was more to the situation he just wasn't telling.

"Before I say I do, is there any reason why you were okay with me asking you last minute to come up here with me?" I expressed, hoping he took heed and told me what was on his mind. I could read it on his face, but I knew his mouth would never utter the words I was looking for.

"Because I love you and I want to be here for your big day," he explained, giving me the best bullshit lie he could muster up. I was going to let him have it because whatever happened in the dark would eventually come to the light. That was for me also.

I heard a knock at the door and knew that it was showtime. If there was any time to back out, it would be before I gave her Champ's money for this updo 360 wig and my soft glam makeup, but I knew in my heart I wasn't going to back out of it.

I placed my plate in the sink and went to open the door for Jasmine. Mike was being an ass because any other time, he would've run to the door, being the protector but all he did was head back to his room. Hopefully, even though he had his opinion, he wouldn't leave me at the altar alone. Other than, Champ he was all I had.

Thinking about Kira, I shot her a text of the place and to make sure that she was still coming. I'd just met her, and she didn't owe me anything to come, but I hoped she did. I wanted to build a friendship with her because she was on familiar grounds that I planned on coming to very soon.

I had waited long enough. It was time for me to get closer to family. I watched so many people's snaps as they went on their girls' trips, and here I was, sitting here, barely wanting to do anything with the few friends I had, but I felt like they were only there because I was beneficial to them. When they needed to borrow anything for a late bill, or they needed me to cover for them in case their mate wanted to know where they were, I was always the fall girl.

Hence, the reason I didn't want them around me on my special day. I would've been paying for my own bachelorette party and what fun would that have been. I'll pass.

Here I was, sitting in the chair after my wash, thinking about everything but the right thing. I should've been happy going to this life and here I was, a bit sad like somebody had died. It was time for me to pep talk myself and get into character. There was nothing wrong with falling back into love with my husband, and that's what I was about to do.

"Are you ready for your big day? Marriage is a beautiful thing," Jasmine questioned, knocking me from my thoughts.

Putting a smile on my face, I responded just like I would to anybody else who'd seen me in my dress today.

"As ready as I'll ever be," I responded to her with a smile. Technically, I wasn't lying telling them that because I truly wasn't going to be anymore ready than I already was.

I sat up in the chair, watching the television as she pulled out all of her material to get to work. Today was my day, and I wasn't about to let anybody mess it up for me. You only said I do for the first time once, and I wanted to make sure that this was my one and only time. Anybody who didn't like it didn't have to be there.

Chapter 20

Champ

I knew the look on Nadia's face after I told her I couldn't come to her room was one of pure disappointment, but I felt like she deserved to know the truth. I could've easily gone with what she asked, but she deserved better from me, and Kira truly deserved for me to be the man she needed me to be.

I had already fucked up sleeping with her the first night I saw her and still, I couldn't get her out of my mind. I was supposed to be thinking about how beautiful my wife was going to be in her dress, not wondering if Nadia had already gone back to wherever she was from.

I had blown every chance that I could've had with her, but it was for the best. In another place or another time, we could've been something but right now, I had to get my mind right on making sure that my wife was happy for the rest of her life.

I still had what Sean said on my mind. I needed to know why Kira was so comfortable with this nigga. I knew she probably would've found somebody to get her get back with, and I had to respect that, but to bring the nigga to Las Vegas where you were about to get married was a different kind of bold.

I knew Kira hadn't lost her mind like that. If she thought she was about to get me to this altar and embarrass me and run off with another man, she had another thing coming. I wasn't a killer, but don't fucking push me. Here I was, thinking these crazy ass thoughts in my head that I needed to get out.

I hadn't talked to Sean since the day we had the argument about Kira. I knew I could have handled things differently, but he'd caught me off guard with the shit he was saying. He should have taken it up with me about having a tail on my girl, even if the tail was him.

He'd voiced his opinion several times about Kira, but he never called her out of her name. No matter what she did or didn't do, I would never let another man disrespect something that belongs to me, friend or not. He knew there were certain lines you didn't cross.

I wasn't about to go running behind the nigga if he wanted to stay gone; it was what it was. If he showed up at the wedding to show his support and be there for me, then I would address the elephant in the room when the time came.

It was also time for me to meet the man who Sean claimed wanted war. As much as I wasn't in the streets, I also knew the minute I helped Sean take the bags from the trap house, his problems became mine. The same way that money helped him get in a better position, it also did the same for me, and I would never forget about how he looked out for me at my lowest.

That's why I hated how things ended with our conversation. We had bumped heads before, but nothing that serious to where we couldn't shake back from it. I was just hoping this time wouldn't be any different. I was also hoping that Kira wasn't the snake he said she was because there was no coming back from it.

I couldn't take what I dished out, and I was man enough to say it. Another part of me questioned if I wanted her to be guilty of the things that were said about her, only to go and try to find Nadia. I was really fucking up.

It was time for me to get up and get ready to marry my soon to be wife. I knew Kira and she wouldn't be anything less than gorgeous. I was just hoping she did the bare minimum with the makeup today, but that would be asking for too much.

I couldn't complain about the little things because there was always going to be something you didn't like about your partner, but if you loved that person the way I loved my fiancée, then you would let it pass.

Seeing my tailored suit hanging on the door, I went to grab it to get this day started. I was just hoping that everything went how it was supposed to because I'd had an eventful time here, but it was time for that to come to an end. I couldn't wait to get my ass back to Vicksburg because I damn sure hoped whatever happened here would stay here.

Chapter 21

Sean

As much as I talked shit to him and he talked shit to me, I still found myself getting ready in my room to have his back. If he wanted to be with a cheater because he cheated, so fucking be it. Who was I to judge anybody? I wasn't nowhere near finding a fucking wife, so it was best I minded my business.

I wouldn't let go of finding out what brought Mike to Las Vegas at the same time we were. That was no coincidence. If he wanted to talk to me like a man and get some shit off his chest, today would be the day.

I had no idea whether he would show up to the wedding like shit was sweet or not. I knew Champ didn't know how he looked, so I needed to be there in case he showed his face. I wanted to get there a little earlier to peep out the seen.

I knew this was a day I was supposed to be happy, on my boy's side, and telling him to fix his damn tie, but this wasn't it for me.

I wondered if Jayda was still here. I never even got the chance to double back and get her information. I liked her vibe and needed a place to get away when it was time to clear my head. I was hoping she would be here after I took care of this because I knew I wouldn't be at this wedding long.

I'd already ordered an Uber to go to the Lakeside Weddings and Events, so it was already waiting when I went downstairs. One thing I knew, even though this event was small, Kira would make sure she spent enough damn money to make it look like his and her whole family were here to see it.

Champ's mother didn't know anything about this, and I knew once she figured out he'd come to Las Vegas to marry Kira without telling her, all hell would break loose, and I didn't want to be the one in the middle of it.

I loved his mother just like she birthed me herself. Maybe he didn't listen to Boosie's song when he told us mama gone tell you when somebody not right.

That was the only thing I could say. I was at fault for calling her out of her name, but she was with the opp, and he knew that didn't sit well with me. She could've been trying to set us up; I didn't know how deep the relationship got and until I knew for sure how far she was involved, it was fuck her and whoever was riding with her.

I knew the driver would charge my card I used on file, so I got out the Uber and headed to the front door. I didn't have to look around long because as soon as I walked in, I saw a sign that said *Welcoming the Champs* with an arrow pointing to where to go. I followed it until it took me outside to a lake. I couldn't lie; this scenery was dope. Her snake ass had some taste, and the people she hired knew exactly what her dream wedding was — boujie and very upscale.

I almost didn't want to sit in the cream seats. I didn't know if they were for decoration or what. I said fuck it and took a seat. I knew by now there was no way for me to be here without them seeing me, so I would just take a seat and see how this shit unfolded.

I must've made it right on time. I turned around when I heard the door opened to see who was coming down. It was crazy to see Jayda and her friend from the hotel heading this way. How the hell did they know Kira? We didn't know who she knew, obviously. I really wanted to see how this was going to go because if I wasn't mistaken, this was the same woman I saw him taking up to her room the first night we came. This couldn't be the woman he was trying to tell me about in the room. If it was, this shit was about to get real, fast. It seemed like all our problems were about to be in the same room at the same time, and nothing good could come of this.

Chapter 21

Nadia

I couldn't lie. My head was still banging from the night before. Champ turning me down had really fucked up my ego. I was back to being the woman who stayed in my own lane and didn't let anyone in.

I was only coming to this wedding because Kira had sent me a text this morning, confirming my attendance, and I was a woman of my word. I was glad I had bought at least one casual outfit, just in case me and Jayda had decided on a brunch date.

I turned around in a circle, admiring my body in the cream romper from Fashion Nova. I had been ready to put it on since it'd been in my closet. I rarely went anywhere, so the romper was just another piece of clothing I bought just to buy. My cream Steve Madden heels paired perfectly with the romper. I wasn't trying to go overboard because Kira had already told me there wasn't going to be a lot of people there. I was just hoping Jayda's ass was ready so we could head to the wedding.

I had my bags packed, ready to put in the car. When we left this wedding, I was saying goodbye to Las Vegas. This weekend had been eventful, but I was ready to get back to my boring life and daycare.

I heard a tap on the door and was praying that was Jayda. The person continued to knock on the door, which let me know that it was her impatient ass. I put my lip gloss on, adding the last little touch, grabbed my suitcase, and headed to the door.

"Damn. Impatient, aren't we?" I muttered, walking out the door.

"You're right. You know I'm not an early person. Especially for somebody I don't even know. I had to get up an hour early to make sure I was ready," she spoke, annoyed, but I didn't care. After this, it was back to the basics.

I didn't even have to tell her to have her bags ready. She was rolling her suitcase just like me.

The place was like fifteen minutes away, so I sat back in the seat and rested my eyes. The first thing that popped into my head was Champ. Opening them again, there was no way I was about to do that to myself; I needed to get myself together and forget about that one night. I was about to go home and for sure treat myself to the money I still had in my purse.

We parked and headed towards the building. I saw a sign that said Welcoming the Champs, so I figured that was the way to go. I had never asked her anything about her husband or their last names, so I was just going with the flow.

Once we followed the signs taking us outside, the scenery blew me. This wedding was goals. The cream and white seats, flowers, and decorations had gone beyond what I expected. I thought she told me many people weren't going to be here, but the way the outside was decorated, you would think over two hundred people would be here.

I felt a tap on my shoulders and turned around to see Jayda looking suspect.

"Bihh, that's him! The guy I had sex with the other night!" she expressed nervously like she didn't want to continue walking.

"Fine time to tell me this story. Now come on, so we can get this over with and head back home."

"I see you're going to be Moody Troody today, so I'm not going to bother you," she proclaimed, and I was fine with it.

Being the petty person I was, out of all the seats, I chose to sit in the row right in front of him just to see her sweat. I knew she wasn't going to sit anywhere else. Laughing to myself, she thought she was slick, holding her head down, but I knew by the look on his face, she was busted.

"So that's what we're doing now, Jayda?" he questioned her, moving to the next seat behind her.

"What do you mean? I didn't see you there," she lied instantly. Just like yesterday when she got a good laugh out of me and Champ, I was about to do the same thing.

"Why are you here? Are you stalking me?" Jayda asked him to try to change the subject.

"Nawl, my best friend is getting married today. This is his wedding. I'm the best man," he told her as Nadia's face changed, looking like she'd seen a ghost.

I turned around, trying to be nosey to see what had gotten her so caught up in her words. I couldn't believe my eyes as I locked eyes with Champ. This was the place he said he had to be today. I guess he was another one of the groomsmen. I turned around quickly, hoping that this would be over soon. I didn't want to see this man again.

Not even stopping by us to speak, he headed straight to the altar. This was starting to feel awkward. Why didn't he address the guy sitting next to me?

"Hey, can I ask you a question?" I asked the guy that Nadia was talking to, but the look she was giving me had already answered my question.

"I don't think you want the answer you're about to ask," he

told me, sitting back in his seat, dismissing my question.

He didn't even know what the hell I was about to ask. The preacher had already made himself to the altar, but the groom and bride still hadn't made it yet. Hearing the music start to play, I could see Kira walking towards the altar.

Seems like forever
That I have waited for you
In a world full of disappointment
One thing is true
God has blessed me
And he's blessed you too
In a world lonely people
I've found you

By now, all of us were on our feet, watching her and a guy walk her down. She looked beautiful but at this moment, I could feel my heart in shambles. I just needed her to confirm what I had come to figure out.

The man that I had grown feelings for was the man she was now standing in front of, holding his hands about to marry. I slowly sat down and knew it wasn't her fault that she had a no-good ass nigga. She was right to feel like she didn't want to get married. A woman's intuition never steered her wrong. I wasn't going to say a word. Karma was going to get his ass back sooner than later.

I knew Jayda was looking over at me, but I didn't want any sympathy. I didn't need it. It seemed like everybody in the room knew what was going on but me and Kira.

Chapter 22

Champ

I walked into my wedding to get into place, and the last face I thought I'd see was sitting front row to my wedding. I tried to tell her so many times, but it wouldn't come out. I knew she deserved to know I was here to get married, but I couldn't tell her. I had grown feelings overnight for this woman, and I didn't want to hurt her feelings, but it seemed like I had done that anyway.

I peeped her turning around fast, so I wouldn't see that she had seen me, but it wasn't a place I could run to not to be seen. My one-night stand was at my wedding, and I was praying even though she didn't owe me anything not to put me on blast.

I heard the music begin and watched as Kira walked down the aisle. I was amazed by the way her dress fitted her and the way she listened to me when I told her not to cake her face up with all that makeup. I wanted to see her beauty shine more today.

As she headed closer and closer to me, I still looked over to try to read Nadia's facial expression, but I couldn't. It was like she had turned her emotions completely off. It wasn't until Nadia stood in front of me that I realized the dude that walked her down was the same guy that tried to pay for my tux.

The shit was about to go bad quick. I knew I had seen him somewhere before, but I couldn't remember exactly where. After letting her hand go, he went to sit directly behind Sean. The way his facial expression had changed, and his hand went towards his hip, I knew some shit was about to go down. I knew Sean like the back of my hand, and he was on go mode. Why the fuck would he go sit right behind Sean?

It was like everything was starting to hit me all at once. I knew Kira didn't have the nigga Sean said she was fucking walk her down the aisle and play in my face. Before I knew it, I had Kira's throat in my hand. I could see the preacher's mouth moving, but nothing he or the Lord said would make me let go of her.

"My nigga, let her go!" I heard the dude, Mike, but I didn't give a fuck about the gun he had pointing at me because I knew there was one pointing right back at him. We would all die here if it came down to it.

"Who the fuck is this nigga to you?" I questioned Kira, letting her neck go just a little so she could answer. Her tears running down her face didn't mean a thing to me. I wanted an answer, and I wanted an answer right fucking now.

"Really, Champ? After all the shit you've put me through. You have the nerve to question me?" As every word came out of Kira's mouth, I knew things wouldn't be the same, no matter how she answered.

"She don't have to answer shit. I think it's about time for y'all to tell me what the fuck y'all do with my money and where the fuck is my product?" he questioned, turning around to be face-to-face with Sean.

"You know them?" Kira asked Mike like she was lost. I didn't know what type of fucking games she was playing.

I decided to let her neck go to see how this unfolded.

"Baby sis, I had no intention to be by your side and support you today. I needed to get as close to these niggas as possible," he told her, but I was lost. How the fuck was this her brother? Let her tell it, she didn't have any family.

"You do know who your family is?" I asked her to try to see

if she would lie to me again. I knew she knew her foster family, but I didn't know anything about her knowing her birth parents. Taking a good look at them, this shit was weird as fuck.

"Fix your face. I haven't gotten to the good part yet. See, you didn't know me, so you wouldn't know that I've been watching you. Let my sister know how the women sitting in the chairs over there are the women you've been with in Las Vegas. I guess what happens in Vegas doesn't stay in Vegas, my nigga."

WANT TO INTERACT WITH T'ANN MARIE & HER TEAM? JOIN OUR READERS GROUPS ON FACEBOOK!

T'ANN MARIE PRESENTS: GRANDMA'S HOUSE | Facebook

T'ANN MARIE PRESENTS: GRANDMA'S HOUSE 2.0 | Facebook

WIN PRIZES, BE APART OF LIVE BOOK DISCUSSIONS & MORE!

Join Our Mailing List:

http://eepurl.com/gU81k5

TMP
Tann Marie
PRESENTS

Are now accepting submissions in the following genres..

URBAN FICTION
URBAN ROMANCE
WOMEN'S FICTION
STREET LITERATURE
URBAN PARANORMAL
BBW URBAN ROMANCE
INTERRACIAL ROMANCE

For consideration, please email the first 5 chapters of your completed manuscript to:

tannmariesubs@gmail.com

Made in the USA
Columbia, SC
28 March 2023